MW01116475

LUNAR CHAOS

by Crystal Rose

Lunar Chaos
By Crystal Rose

Book Cover by Creative Digital Studios

Illustrations by Tinah Ferreira

First edition 2023

Dedication
To all the survivors out there.

"You've been who you are to survive, now let yourself be the person who thrives." - author unknown

Acknowledgments

Thank you to my amazing editor Sloan! You are an amazing human and I'm so happy to have you in my life!

Thank you to my readers. You have no idea how much joy it brings me when you relate to my characters or find an escape in my books. You all are incredible!

Thank you to my sisters for always being there for me and supporting me.

Sensitivity reader statement

I did have a hormonally intersex person read my manuscript. They found my writing of an intersex character to be respectful and well done.

"I think Latisha being an intersex character is handled respectfully and done well as far as my experience goes"

I unfortunately was not able to find second intersex sensitivity reader like I wanted to within my indie author budget for this book. I deeply apologize if you find any of the material in this book offensive. My goal was to respectfully write an intersex main character in my story.

To research for this book I watched content made by intersex creators about their experiences as intersex people. I also read through the information on the ineractadvocates.org website.

CRYSTAL ROSE

PROLOGUE

Latisha

CW: child abuse, drug abuse, suffering from drug addiction, physical harm inflicted on a child, portrayal of income insecurity

There is a summary of the prologue at the beginning of chapter 1 for all my readers who would prefer to skip this section due to the content warning.

I rummaged through the kitchen cabinets looking for food. Cabinet after cabinet they were all empty. Mom hadn't been buying as much food for us lately, but there was always *something* to eat, until today that is.

I went into her bedroom and found her napping per usual. Even in the bright afternoon sun, her skin looked a sickly ashen blue. She worked and napped and worked and napped. Then every once in a while she'd buy me a bunch of food, leave the apartment, and I wouldn't see her for sun cycles on end. I'd learned to ration the food she gave me when she left, but she wasn't gone. She was right there and there was still no food.

"Momma," I shook her shoulder. "Momma,

wake up." She groaned and rolled over in bed. I shook her other shoulder, "Momma, there's no food."

"Hmm?" She groaned again.

"There's no food to eat," I repeated.

"There's no money. Have to pay off debt," she said in a sleepy tone.

"Momma, what debt?" I shook her shoulder again. I was a youngling, but I was old enough to gather that the male called Bogden was probably the Sirret she owed credits to. Sometimes momma was super happy to see him. He gave her what looked like a medical inhaler, and shortly after that was when she'd leave for day cycles on end. But sometimes when he came around momma would tell me to hide in my bedroom and lock the door. I'd hear him yell at her and she'd say *I'm sorry* over and over again, and *I'll get you the credits, I promise.*

When momma didn't respond I left her room and decided to watch the entertainment feed to get my mind off the hunger gnawing at my belly. A loud knock at the door made me jump. I put my buzzpad down on the table and opened the door. Bogden stood on the stoop looking angry.

"Where is she," he snarled. I had only just opened the door and he was already scaring me. I took a step back and tried to push the button to close the door again, but he grabbed my hand before I could.

"Your mom owes me credits, a lot of them." He frowned and shoved his way past me. He walked straight for momma's bedroom. I grabbed onto his leg to try and slow him down, but he just shook me off. I was only nine years old, and very small for my age, so it wasn't hard for him to do.

He pushed the door open and started yelling at momma.

"Where are my credits, you trash!"

Momma jumped out of bed. "I'll get them to you. I just made a payment yesterday. It might take a while, but I'll get you the credits I owe."

"You said you'd pay me back in full in two weeks. You begged me for one more inhaler of haze, and I gave it to you. That was four weeks ago." He slapped her across the face. Her eyes were wide as she touched the dark blue mark on her cheek.

"You don't hurt my momma," I yelled and started kicking him as hard as I could.

"Ow! You little brat!" He grabbed me by the arm and held me away from him. He acted like he was about to throw me when an awful grin spread across his face. It was a wicked grin full of bad ideas.

"I think I've just thought of the perfect solution. You say you don't have the credits to pay me back, but I see a shipload of credits right here." He grabbed one of my horns. "You know how much a Sirret's horns are worth these days?"

"No. Let go of her!" Momma walked toward me, but he shoved her back against the wall.

"There's a planet one galaxy over that has discovered a way to make a powerful drug out of horns from all kinds of species. Bullhog horns, tork horns, mushra horns, and even Sirret horns."

I didn't understand what he was talking about.

How could a Sirret's horns be worth anything? Did they cut off the horns of the elderly after they died? I imagined Bogden sneaking into a medic clinic and cutting off the horns of a dead patient.

Bogden rifled through his pockets looking for something.

"I heard they pay one hundred thousand credits per horn and seeing as we don't have any horned animals on Ozinda, my only option is to take a poor Sirret's horns, perhaps the horns of the daughter of a Sirret who owes me lots of credits."

"No!" Momma lunged for me again, and again he threw her against the wall.

"Stay down!" he yelled and pointed a finger at momma, who was already trying to get up again. "Stay down, and I'll give you two inhalers before I leave, one for each horn. Then we'll be even."

She looked back and forth between me and Bogden, eyes wide with indecision.

"Momma," I pleaded. I understood what was happening now. Bogden didn't intend on taking the horns of dead Sirrets, he planned on taking my horns while I was very much still alive.

She looked at Bogden with resignation in her eyes and sat back down. She glanced at me one last time then looked down at the floor.

"Momma!" I reached out for her, but she didn't move. She just kept sitting there looking at the ground.

"Good," Bogden grunted. He rifled through his pockets some more until he found what he was looking for.

I heard him flip a switch and then there was a light humming that drew closer to my head.

"What is that," I breathed. Panic started to set in as the reality of what was happening really hit me. I'd only ever seen one other person without a horn, and they lost it in a factory accident. Everyone looked at him like he was ugly and diseased. I didn't want that. I just wanted to get out of here.

"Just hold still. This will all be over soon." I tried wiggling out of his grasp but he only held onto me tighter. "If you move my laser is going to cut right through your skull. I don't want to kill you, but I will if you don't stop moving," he seethed.

I held still. I wasn't ready to die. I didn't want to lose my horns either, but with momma just sitting there like that what could I do? I couldn't believe she'd stopped fighting for me.

I heard the hum of the laser drawing closer again. Then the hum turned into a sizzling sound like plastic popping and melting. Before I knew it one of my horns landed on the floor with a thud. It wasn't the whole horn, but it was most of it. Moments later the other horn dropped onto the floor next to it, and just like that my life had completely changed

Bogden let go of me. I stood up straight and nearly fell over. My head was too light. I felt off balance. I looked over at momma. She was crying now, but she still wouldn't look up, she wouldn't stand, she wouldn't fight, she wouldn't do anything. She'd chosen to not protect me, and I couldn't understand why.

Suddenly the room felt too small and I needed to get out of there. I ran outside onto the street and kept running. I ran into a building not knowing what it was and I found myself in the middle of a bar full of rowdy males. A fight had broken out, and I had to duck and crawl to get past everyone.

There were some cabinets along the lower half of the wall. I opened one and found that it was empty. A male with a bloody nose fell directly behind me. I crammed my small body into the cabinet and closed the door. My head hit the top and I ducked to make room for my horns. Then it dawned on me that if I still had my horns I would have never been able to fit in here. I would still be out there, trying not to get hit.

I touched the top of my head and felt the empty space where my horns had been. It felt strange and unfamiliar. I didn't like it, but in that moment I was grateful that my lack of horns gave me the ability to hide and find safety.

Eventually, the fighting ended. I stayed in the cabinet for the rest of the day and well into the evening. Once I heard the bartender leave and lock the door behind him, I came out from my hiding spot. The room was dark but the moon shining through the windows gave me enough light to see by. I looked through the cold storage under the bar and found boxes of fresh fruit and some crackers. I ate the bowl of fruit and held the box of crackers under my arm. I had finally eaten my first meal of the day, and I already had enough food for tomorrow in my hands.

I couldn't fall asleep here. I was afraid if I did, the bartender might come in early and see me there. No, I needed to go somewhere else. I pushed the button to open the door. Once I left the building the door shut and locked behind me. I looked down the street and nothing really stuck out to me as a safe place to go. I sighed and decided to go back home. Bogden wouldn't be there anymore, and even though I couldn't trust my mother, my bedroom door did at least have a lock on it.

I walked in the door to the apartment and momma immediately stood up and walked toward me. She went to hug me, but a split second before she did so I saw a flash of horror in her eyes as she looked at my hornless head for the first time.

"Latisha, I'm so glad you're home! I've been looking everywhere for you!" She wrapped her arms around me and I stood there motionless. She withdrew herself from me and we just stared at each other for a long moment. I tried to think of something to say but no words came to mind. What could I say? *How could you? Why didn't you help me?* None of that mattered anymore. What was done was done. I walked past her to my room and locked the door behind me.

I continued to sleep at my mother's apartment every night. I wouldn't say I lived there because I didn't. As soon as I woke up in the morning I would head straight for the door and leave. I learned how to steal food with the other street younglings.

"You're a natural," a youngling commented.

"Yeah, I have no idea how you can fit in such small spaces." Another youngling stated. I had stolen a cloak and always wore my hood up. No one knew I had lost my horns. I learned how to move in the shadows, how to be silent and swift. I learned how to survive.

It wasn't too long after the incident that momma started using the inhalers Bogden gave her at home. I learned those inhalers had a drug in them called haze. They helped momma feel happy. One night I came home to her on the floor. She had thrown up and she was shivering. I shook her shoulder but she didn't respond.

I pressed the button on the door that alerted the medics of an emergency and sat next to her while I waited for them to arrive.

"Latisha," momma groaned and held out her hand. I took her hand in mine. It was so cold, as if all her blood had left her body.

"I'm so sorry," she whispered. "I should have protected you."

All the words I wanted to say were again caught in my throat. I hated her, and I wanted to yell at her, but she was also the same momma who took care of me for most of my life. The same momma who sang me to sleep, and built blanket forts with me. A part of me wanted to tell her it wasn't her fault, but it was her fault. She could have chosen me, she could have at least tried to protect me, but she didn't. So I sat there, held her hand, and said nothing.

Was I at fault here? If I had never trusted

momma in the first place, would I have my horns still? I could have been out looking for food this morning, but instead, I was at home trusting that my mom would take care of me.

"Don't let anyone take advantage of you, Latisha. Don't trust anyone."

Those were the last words she spoke to me before the medics arrived. They hauled her off to the medic clinic where she later died.

Don't trust anyone. Her words echoed through my head. *I won't momma.* I made a vow that day that I'd never trust anyone again.

Prologue summary

Latisha's mom struggles with substance abuse. She gets in over her head and owes her drug dealer money.

The drug dealer demands payment and explains that Sirret horns can sell for a lot of credits.

He proceeds to cut off Latisha's horns with a laser cutter. Latisha's mom just sits there and does nothing. Latisha feels betrayed by her mother.

Latisha stops depending on her mom and becomes more independent. Shortly after all this her mother dies and Latisha vows never to trust anyone again.

List of content warnings:
child endangerment
injury of a child
stabbing

attempted sexual assult
torture via a medical device
sexually explicit scenes
portrayal of economic insecurity
conversations about infertility

CHAPTER 1

Latisha
Scroll one page back for summary of the prologue.

Clink, clink, clink, every plate I set on the table clinked on the clear glass surface. Monstair Kach, the old honorific for a merchant which Kach insisted on using, was hosting a rutting dinner tonight. Kohner from house Zelell and Larris from house Rasmux would be joined by their rut specialists tonight for a five-course meal. Whoever lasted the longest without having to leave to satisfy their needs won. In true merchant-class fashion, there was no prize, just the bragging rights that one house was stronger than the other.

The servant woman across from me wore a gray apron over a plain white smock. The apron matched the bandana covering her long white hair. The male servants wore plain gray shirts and trousers. I wore the same outfit as the woman across from me. I wasn't usually a fan of uniforms, but the bandana did make it easier for me to blend in with my broken horns.

The dining room was quiet except for the soft

music playing in the background and the clinking of the plates and utensils as we set them on the table. Once we finished our task of setting the table the servant woman and I reentered the kitchen.

I was hit with humid air, the scent of fresh spiced stew, the banging of pots and pans, and Rali, the head kitchen servant yelling her orders to the other servants. I enjoyed the noise and commotion of the kitchen. It was easier to slip into the background and not be noticed here.

"Alright Layla," Layla was the alias I'd given when I was hired at house Dinak, Monstair Kach's residence. I wasn't exactly famous as a stealth agent, but sometimes my real name paired with my broken horns did give me away. Kach was the owner and Monstair of the estate and its wealth. His parents had died not too long ago, leaving him in charge of everything.

"Now that you're done with the table settings, I need you to fill the wine glasses. Get the gwava berry wine from the cellar, but wait until everyone is seated before you start pouring. They like their wine fresh from the bottle."

As the newest hire to House Dinak, Rali was giving me detailed instructions for what to do while serving my first dinner here. I made my way downstairs to the cellar and brought up two bottles of wine. I then walked back through the kitchen and peeked out the door into the dining room. Kach was sitting at the table with his guests. He had his hands steepled in front of him in the way he did when he had stopped listening to the conversation and was just waiting for his turn to speak.

The two men had pinched looks of pain on their faces, which was to be expected. The rut specialists, a woman in a skin-tight red body suit and a shirtless man in tight black pants, were doing their best to look interested in the stuffy conversation.

I opened the bottle of wine, took a deep breath, and walked into the dining room.

"And I said, what's it to you? Your factory hasn't made more than one hundred thousand GDP in over five years!" The rut specialists laughed at Kach's joke, but the sour expressions on the faces of the rutting males didn't change. He saw me approach and leaned back in his chair, giving me room to pour his wine.

I moved from person to person, filling their cups. Through the clear glass table, the large bulges in the pants of the two rutting males were obvious. I had a little sympathy for them, every Sirret person does. A rut is hard enough to deal with in the privacy of your own home let alone at a formal dinner. Given my unique biology as an allgender person with both male and female hormones, I had one rut every six months as the males did, but my rut only lasted for one day as a females would. This dinner was a stark reminder that my rut was coming up soon and I was not looking forward to it.

Out of the corner of my eye, I spotted a bodyguard I hadn't seen before. My only interactions with Kach had been serving him breakfast in the formal dining room, and his morning guards, Gunok and Cruun, had been the ones attending to him. This male was an interesting mixture of what looked like a human and a Katsuro with his distinctly human face, cat ears, furry arms, pawed feet, and a Katsuro tail.

His brown and orange fur was well suited for the dark green and gold Dinak uniform he wore. It was interesting that he chose to not wear any foot coverings. They made boots for pawed feet. Perhaps he performed his duties better without them. The end of his tail laid limp on the floor and I wondered if it was as sensitive as a Sirret tail. It looked so soft, so touchable.

"Female, more wine." Larris waved his empty glass in the air. I walked to his side of the table and felt the gaze of the human Katsuro guard following me. His formerly limp tail now twitched back and forth.

Kach started a long-winded speech about tradition and strong warrior males throughout the centuries. The rutting males weren't paying attention and the rut specialists looked bored. Another servant entered the room with a fresh bottle of wine once mine was empty, which was my cue to go back to the kitchen for more instructions from Rali.

"Ten credits on me bedding Airna before the end of the week." I entered the kitchen in the middle of a heated debate.

"I'll take that wager. Ten credits says I'm going to bed her before you do."

"Neither of you fools are going to bed Airna. Now stop talking about her like a prize instead of the proud Sirret that she is and start chopping these vegetables before I throw you both out onto the street!" Rali was all harsh words with no teeth to back them up. She wouldn't hurt a small house beetle let alone throw anyone out into the street. Even I knew that and I'd only been here a week. No, from what I'd observed everyone followed her directives because they respected her, much like how the security team followed Jaris because we respected him.

"I see Bowen is on duty today. He may look strange, but the male has talent." Bexi a Sirret woman in her late twenties like me, peeked out the door to take another look at the dining room.

"How so?" I couldn't help but ask. I was as intrigued by him as everyone else.

"I overheard the guards talking about how he took out 4 henchmen from a rival house all on his own. He returned without a scratch on him. He's a slippery male despite all that fur."

"Is he Katsuro?" I couldn't help but ask. I wanted to know more about this guard.

"He's Katsuro and human. He said some scientists enhanced his genetics by mixing his genes with Katsuro genes."

Bexi looked back out at the dining room then turned back to the kitchen to call out, "They're ready for the soup!"

Bexi, Yariletta, and I lined up to grab one tray each from the soup chef. Each tray had two bowls of spiced tuber soup, except for my tray which had one bowl specifically for Kach. We filed into the room and placed the bowls in front of the guests and host.

"Thank you," Kach rumbled deep in his throat. He grazed one finger over my forearm as I placed his bowl in front of him. I shivered at his touch. This man may be Jaris' friend, but there was something off about him.

"Dinner has begun," Kach announced. "My servants make the finest food in all of Ozinda. Just last week I gave them all a bonus for their hard work."

"Yeah, right after he reduced our pay the week before because he said we were all lazy." I walked into the kitchen past Drav, a young male servant who didn't really have any reason to be in the kitchen right now other than to see all the drama. He wasn't the only one though. There were a group of servants hovering around the kitchen island taking bets.

"Twenty credits that house Zelell wins." Vinee, who I'd been following since Drannon spotted him with a messenger bot going to Kach's house, declared.

"No way, did you see the guy from house Rasmux? He looks like he has the self-control of a stone."

"Looks can be deceiving, and there's a lot at play here. One look at their specialist might have them crumbling like a dried leaf under my boot."

"Twenty credits on house Zelell." I chimed in.

"Hey hey! Layla joining the fun!" Emed patted my back as if we were best friends and not as if he thought he was about to win my credits.

"I like you. You're quiet, keep to yourself, and know how to spend your credits." Vinee gave me a toothy grin as he counted my money and added it to the growing pile.

"I want in too!" A petulant youngling demanded. I could barely see their horns over the kitchen island.

"Get out of here! You don't even have twenty credits to bet." Vinee shooed the child away.

"They're ready for the main course," Bexi yelled.

Yariletta, Bexi, and I grabbed the trays of food and headed out the door.

"You say one more thing about house Zelell and I'll cut your throat!" Kohner was standing and pointing a finger at Larris.

Quickly as I could, I put Kach's plate in front of him.

"It's alright, the food's here." The male rut specialist cajoled Kohner. "Just sit down and eat." He rubbed Kohner's back gently up and down and Kohner's eyes nearly popped out of his head at the touch. Then the male started to purr.

"Bif me!" he backhanded the shirtless rut specialist. "What are you, stupid?!"

I tried to walk past them as quickly as possible but as I passed him Kohner growled and shoved his wine and food off the table. Unfortunately, it all landed on me. I gazed at Bowen as he flinched and balled his fist. He looked ready to fight. Bexi and Yariletta froze for the briefest of moments before walking on either side of me and ushering me out of the dining room.

"Come on, let's go," the defeated man grumbled

on his way out.

Back in the kitchen, everyone was quiet as we entered the room. It was unsettling to see so many people stand still while they stared at you. Then, like a tidal wave of sound, hoots and hollers erupted all around me.

"Welcome to house Dinak! You don't really belong until a guest throws something at you." Emed smiled and clapped his hands, welcoming me to the serving team.

Rali put an arm around my shoulder and led me to the servant's back stairwell. Other servants patted my back as we walked past. I bristled at the attention and affection. I wasn't used to such treatment and it was unsettling. *This is just a job, Latisha. You have to play the part*, I reminded myself and forced myself to relax.

"Now go on upstairs and get cleaned up and changed. You did well tonight Layla, you'll be a great addition to the staff here." I smiled at the kind female's words and shuffled out from under her arm. Once free of her motherly affection I ran up the stairs, trying to get away from everyone's overwhelming kindness as soon as I could.

CHAPTER 2

Bowen

My tail thumped on the floor as I tried to relax in bed. I was still getting used to my tail. It was nice to have the added balance, but the dang thing seemed to have a mind of its own. I looked out the window and tried to forget that I was not back home cursing the bugs and all the noise they made in the heat of summer. But the view was too different. There was a big ass moon taking up half the sky and a space station whose blinking lights never stopped flashing.

Those fucking alligator men just had to snatch me out of my bed. They couldn't have picked anyone else in the whole damn U.S. of A. I guess it wasn't all bad. I may not have liked the process of getting this altered body, and those scientists and their ticking medical equipment would haunt my dreams for the rest of my days. But I had to admit... it had its benefits. I could pick a scent out of a crowd and hear a conversation over fifty feet away. I could leap great distances and jump down from tall buildings without getting hurt. I was a real specimen of scientific ingenuity. If the scientists had any motivation other than seeing how far they could push genetics, I might consider their accomplishment noble. But seeing as how all they wanted to do was play god, I'll continue to hate them until the day I die.

"Yes…just like that." I heard two men going at it in the bed beside mine. The living quarters here were less than ideal. There were eight of us men sharing one room crammed with old beds and lumpy pillows.

"Would you keep it down over there?" I chastised them. I was in no mood to be kept awake by the sounds of my roommates pleasuring each other.

"Why don't you come join us Bowen? I'll play with your tail." My roommate's voice was full of seductive promise.

"Why don't you just keep your moanin' and gruntin' to yourselves." I had nothing against men having sex with other men. As a bisexual myself I had enjoyed both men and women over the years, but ever since those scientists altered my genes with one of those cat people, I couldn't get hard. It'd been six months since they finished up with me and still, my cock remained as soft as a wet noodle.

In all my thirty-two years I'd never struggled with such a problem, but now with a whole galaxy full of beautiful people, I couldn't partake in the joys of sensual pleasure with anyone. Not even thinking about that new servant woman did the trick, and boy was she fine, looking like a cool treat on a hot summer day.

I could have punched that man for throwing

food at her like that. But I had to cool my jets as I was under contract for the next five years to work for Kach, who expected me to hold my temper at bay. When the scientists were done poking and prodding me like a fucking lab rat, Kach bought me to join his ranks of personal bodyguards. Legally, my contract says I'm a free man who's just paying off a debt, but in reality, I'm Kach's slave. And if I ever try to leave before my five years are up I could be sentenced to a lifetime in prison.

I've been here for about six months, and I've made a bit of a reputation for myself as uninterested, unbothered, and not to be messed with. And yes from time to time I've been known to be a bit of a grump. I've become a civil acquaintance to almost everyone in the house and that was how I'd like to keep things, civil.

The grunting and moaning in the bed next to mine came to a fever pitch, and then I was met with blissful silence. Now I might finally get some sleep.

❈ ❈ ❈

Latisha

The next day I smoothed out the blanket on the bed in the guest room and dusted the places the bots couldn't reach. I checked the room one more time before I was satisfied that everything was clean. Then I peeked out the door to see if anyone was in the hallway. It was quiet and empty, not a Sirret to be seen.

So I silently made my way across the hall to Kach's room.

His owner suite was a massive open space. His bedroom led to his private living room, then to a small dining area, and finally a door that opened to a veranda. On silent feet, I walked to his bedroom and opened every drawer, closet, and cabinet searching for anything that would clue me in on how much Kach really knew about this rebellion.

I was looking behind a picture frame mounted to the wall and spied a hidden vault. *Yes.* I silently celebrated. Then I heard a voice from behind me. "Hello there, sweetheart. Now, what might you be up to?" A male voice purred.

Sweet heart? Was this male threatening to eat me? I calmed my nerves and slowly turned to face whomever this foe might be. It was the guard from last night, Bowen, he stood there in a dark green uniform with a phase gun and a variety of knives and daggers holstered to his belt.

"Do not comment on the tastiness of my organs, you barbarian." The audacity of this male, who didn't even know me, in threatening to taste my organs. He wasn't one to be underestimated, that was for sure.

The right side of his mouth curved up in a smirk. "I believe there's been a misunderstanding. I am not commenting on your internal organs, but you, however, do seem to be avoiding my question." He raised an eyebrow as if to indicate he'd bested me.

"I'm just cleaning. It's not an offense to be

thorough in cleaning Monstair Kach's room."

"It wouldn't be if Cassia hadn't already cleaned it an hour ago." He folded his arms over his chest and his mouth stretched with another smug smirk.

When I didn't respond he let out a deep sigh and continued. "Why don't you go be thorough somewhere else, sweetheart, and I promise not to speak of your little intrusion into Monstair Kach's room to anyone."

"Whatever you say, barbarian." I shoulder-checked him as I left the room, and when I was far away from his prying eyes I inspected the dagger I stole from his belt. That barbarian might think he'd bested me, but he'd soon learn I always had the last word.

* * *

Bowen

That woman was gonna be trouble, I could tell already. I thought to myself as I waited outside my uncertified medic's door and tried not to itch at the hives that were all over my body. My altered genetics made me allergic to everything, and if I didn't get an allergy shot once every two weeks, I wound up an itching mess.

Krix's door finally opened. "Come on in, make yourself comfortable while I get your meds ready." She left the door open and walked into the back room where she kept all her medicine. I went in and pulled the door shut behind me, taking a seat on the metal table. It was clearly meant for surgery but her living room didn't have the space to have a padded chair *and* a metal surgery table. It was clear she'd opted for the more important of the two, and seeing as her patients were going to come to her whether she made them comfortable or not, that made sense.

Her walls were lined with neatly organized medical supplies and monitors. The space was overall very tidy despite it being so small.

"Alright, you know what to do." Krix walked in with a tool that resembled an airport security wand but was, instead, a medical scanner that projected onto the wall. I come here because Krix doesn't use the expensive hospital-grade equipment. The scientists had used that shit. The vitals monitor was the worst of it. Instead of a soft beep like we had on the monitors on Earth, those fuckers had monitors that tick. *Tick, tick, tick,* a horrible high-pitched sound that had grated on my nerves, and brought me to the edge of insanity. Now if I hear a ticking sound, my hair stands on end, my heart feels like it's beating outside of my chest, and I get an irrepressible urge to run. There were no vitals monitors here in Krix's living room, just cheap medical scanners, which was fine by me.

"See you later, my beautiful mate." Krager, a tattoo artist and Krix's wife, walked past us, pausing to exchange a kiss. Then she continued on her way out the door, munching on a piece of fruit

"Bye, love! Have a good day," Krix yelled.

"I will! See you later!" The door shut and Krix

turned her attention back to me.

"What brings you in, the usual?" She held a light to my eyes and examined my pupils.

"Yes, ma'am. My hives are back."

"It's a shame what those scientists did to you. I'm surprised all that gene splicing didn't do more harm than just some severe allergies."

"Oh, I don't know, having severe allergies to nearly everything feels pretty bad to me."

"You should thank the goddess you don't have it worse than you do." She eyed me critically as if I had offended her by not being more grateful for my plight.

"I didn't pay no heed to the gods of my home planet, and I'm not about to give gratitude to the goddess of this one. Besides, what have any of them done for me? I ain't had nothing but suffering my whole life."

"Maybe you'd have a little less suffering if you *did* give the goddess some gratitude." She lifted the med stick to my neck and I tilted my head to the side to receive the injection.

"Oh, like you, working out of your living room because you can't afford to finish medical school?"

Krix slapped my shoulder. "Don't be rude." She was right to slap me. I shouldn't have said what I did, especially in her own home.

"Yes, ma'am. I'm sorry for my curtness. I just don't have much to be grateful for these days, or any of the days prior." I bowed my head in apology.

"I understand the feeling. Just don't give up hope. Something good might be just around the corner." I opened my mouth to make a comment about how I've searched every corner on Ozinda already, but it didn't feel appropriate.

"Thank you for your sympathy, Dr. Krix." I said instead.

"It's just Krix." She gave me a weak smile. I knew it ate at her that she'd probably never have that title even though she had all the skills for it. Just another way the upper class kept the lower class in poverty. You had to have money to make money, and most of us on Ozinda didn't have any money.

"Thank you all the same." I gave her my best southern gentleman grin.

"Is there anything else that's been bothering you?" She asked as she put her supplies away.

"Other than feeling numb both inside and out, I don't have any complaints."

"What do you mean, numb?" Her eyebrows scrunched together in a confused look.

"You know, like all the emotions have been sucked out of my brain, and all I feel is numb." That was except for the few times I'd had to kill someone on Kach's orders. It was disturbing how alive *that* made me feel, and I tried not to think about it.

"That's normal for people here. Living in the slums or serving in a merchant's house will do that to you." She said as she continued to put supplies away on her shelves.

"No, it's different than that. I've been poor my whole life. Hell, I've been poorer than poor, but I never felt like *this*. This feels like my brain chemistry is off."

"Hmm, interesting. I don't have any psychological meds here. It's not my speciality. But I'd guess that the gene splicing may have had an effect on your emotions, too."

"Yeah, I figured that. I'll just have to live with it for a while." I paid her the credits I owed and headed out the door.

CHAPTER 3

Latisha

My stomach growled as I looked down at my bowl of soup. Dinner in the servant's hall was never really enough to satisfy a person's hunger. The soup that sat in front of me could stand to have more noodles in it. At least I also had a piece of bread and a mug of tea. The mug was a unique design that curved inward so it was more comfortable to hold. When I ate my first dinner here I was surprised at how nice the servant's mugs were until I noticed the chip at the top; then I saw that every mug was chipped. Kach must have gotten the whole lot on clearance because why would he actually spend credits on his servants?

As more people sat down at the long table, I looked up to see who had joined us. The lighting was dim, making it hard to see, and the air was cold and musty which sent a shiver down my spine. The servant's hall was in the basement next to the wine cellar, and I'd been told that we were lucky that we had a servant's hall at all. Dirgach didn't provide a place for his servants to eat. He wouldn't even give them a table outside they had to buy one themselves.

"Hey Bexi, are you going to dance with me at the servant's ball coming up?" Emed's mouth was turned up in a grin as if his request would obviously be met with an affirmative.

"I don't know." Bexi gave him a sultry smile as she stirred her soup. "It depends on how nice you treat me this week."

"Oh I'll treat you real nice," he smiled as he shifted in his seat, adjusting himself. Bexi rolled her eyes and continued to eat her soup.

"Attention! Attention! An announcement from Merchant Dirgach is about to commence!" A male voice blasted through every person's buzzpad at the same time. The voice was slightly distorted since it was coming from so many devices at once, giving it a menacing tone.

Everyone at the table groaned. These announcements were propaganda intended to make the lower class feel better about their terrible jobs and low wages.

"Hello, this is Dirgach speaking. I wanted to join you around your dinner table tonight and commend you all for the great and honorable work you do serving in the merchant houses, the factories, fields, and mines. This society thrives because of your great work…"

As he continued to drone on I couldn't help but think about how his own servants were listening to this at a table they had to buy themselves. How could he speak about our commendable work when he wouldn't even buy a biffing dinner table for his own servants? All of the merchants were terrible people, but Dirgach was the worst of them all.

The message cut off after his final words and we were left in an eerie silence.

"There's no one worse than him on Ozinda, I can tell you that." Emed looked down at his buzzpad as if he could still see Dirgach's face on it.

"They're all like that, it's just Dirgach is the most open about his actions," Venpan, the longest-serving servant of Kach spoke up.

"It's about time we rise up then. We shouldn't have to take this anymore," Vinee added from the other side of the table.

"We should retaliate for what they did to the warehouse," Emed huffed.

"My Ryla almost died in that fire. If it weren't for his mate, our friend Drannon would have died too." Cassia held her little daughter close to her as if she was feeling the fear of losing her all over again.

"That human did a brave thing for being one so small." Venpan placed his hand over Cassia's.

"Bravery comes in all shapes and sizes." Cassia held her head up high as if Claire's victory in saving Drannon were her own.

"That it does." Venpan withdrew his hand and gave Cassia a bashful smile.

Cassia got lucky. In my experience, no one ever put their life on the line for anyone, no matter how close they were. I'd survived this long because I only depended on myself.

Vinee looked around the room cautiously then leaned in to whisper to everyone at the table. "The Junak has something planned. I got orders just this morning to be ready to mount an attack in half a moon orbit or less."

"Who or what are we attacking?" Emed looked eager for a fight.

"I don't know yet. As soon as I get the information I'll pass it along." Vinee leaned back and ran a hand through his hair, trying to look calm and collected.

The door to the basement squeaked open and a moment later I saw the Barbarian descending the stairs. He carried a bowl of soup and a mug, and his orange and brown tail swished behind him. He had unbuttoned the collar of his uniform and I could see the top of his chest. I unconsciously licked my lips as if he were a tasty treat I'd like to snack on. I shook my head clear of those thoughts. I wasn't going to taste anyone while working this job, least of all him.

"Welcome! We were just discussing the rebellion." Vinee eyed Bowen as if he were assessing a threat. Bowen was the only guard who ate with the rest of the servants. Guards were considered higher class than servants, and didn't associate with them unless they had to. So it was strange that Bowen ate his dinner with us and I wondered what his motivation was for doing so.

"What do you say, catman? Do you like working for the enemy? Do you enjoy protecting the Monstair with your life?" Vinee leaned back in his chair, trying to look calm, but his thrashing tail betrayed him.

Bowen put his bowl and mug down on the table and sat directly across from me. He looked entirely unphased. "I don't work for Kach, I get paid by him, just like you."

"Not just like me. I clean and maintain Kach's volt car, I don't protect the male from actual harm." Vinee seethed.

"Volt car, Monstair–they're both just jobs, they both pay money. I might protect Kach, but I'm not loyal to him." Bowen was as relaxed as ever as if they were speaking about the weather and not his loyalty to the rebellion.

"So you're loyal to the rebellion then?"

"Now, I didn't say that. I'm loyal to myself." He ate a spoonful of soup and didn't even look down the table at Vinee.

"Sounds like a lonely existence," Venpan added.

"It's one that works for me." Bowen looked up and glanced at me before he returned to his soup.

"What about you, Layla?" Emed asked. "You've been here for a week now and haven't said a word about the rebellion."

"That's because I consider it dangerous to talk about the rebellion with people I barely know." I kept my tone even and took a sip of my tea. I don't want to come off as anything but an aloof female servant who was a safe person for everyone to share their secrets with.

"Well you know us now. You can talk freely. No one here will run their mouth about ya," Vinee encouraged.

I was here to gather intel from these people, and they were more likely to give me information if I said I was on their side. "I'm on the side of the people. I stand with the rebellion." My tone was firm and resolute and I was met with curt nods of approval from almost everyone at the table. It seemed I'd made the right decision.

Pleased with how the conversation had gone, I went back to eating my soup. It was blander than I liked so I reached for the spice shaker. I wrapped my fingers around it and just as I was about to lift it off the table I felt someone wrap their fingers around mine. I looked up and saw Bowen had also reached for the shaker.

"After you, sweetheart." He removed his hand from mine and the corner of his mouth quirked up.

This male was so irritating. Usually my glares and cold personality were enough to keep people away when I didn't want to be bothered, but this male seemed to take it as a challenge. Maybe I'd just have to try harder to get him to not like me.

I finished using the shaker and looked up and down the table. "Here Cassia, do you need the spice shaker?" I handed the shaker down the table to Cassia before she could even answer.

"Thanks! I guess my soup could use a bit more flavor."

I glanced at Bowen who was looking mildly annoyed.

"Ms. Cassia, can you pass the spice back down

here when you're done with it."

"Sure thing." Cassia leaned over and whispered to Bexi, "What's a miss?"

"I don't know. It's another one of his strange human words that don't translate," Bexi whispered back.

Cassia passed the shaker back down the table, but before Bowen could reach it, I snatched it up again.

"Sorry, I think I need this one more time." I shook some more seasoning onto my soup then passed the shaker down the other way. "Here Emed, your soup looks a little bland." Emed smiled and took the shaker.

Bowen leaned back, crossed his arms over his chest, and pinned me with an annoyed glare. "Is there a reason you're so against me having some spice with my meal?"

"I don't know what you're talking about." I shrugged my shoulders and tried very hard not to make eye contact. I was afraid I'd give myself away with a mischievous smile if I did.

"Right, well sweetheart if you're done passing the salt to everyone else at the table, I would really like the chance to season my food."

"I didn't realize barbarians needed seasoning." I dared a glance at his direction. He was looking mildly perturbed with a small hint of a grin.

"You declared I was a barbarian, not me." His grin grew a bit wider. Why was he grinning?

"If you say so." This time when the shaker came back down the table I didn't stop Bowen from receiving it. He shook it a few times, stirred his soup and ate another spoonful.

"Now, that's much better." He set the spice down on the table in front of me. "Just in case you want to pass it down to anyone else." His grin was wide now, and I was more irritated than ever. Somehow my attempt to push him away seemed to have made him more interested than before. Bif me.

CHAPTER 4

Bowen
CW: stabbing

The cool morning breeze ruffled my hair as I stood on the rooftop across from a nondescript building. I was given orders by Kach himself to stand guard and wait for a young Sirret male with a Junak helmet tattoo to bring a messenger bot to this building. I was also told that if anyone should harm the young man, I was to come to his aid.

I stood there for most of the morning, long enough to see the sun go from barely a whisper of light to the full brightness of the noon day. Only a few people had passed through this mostly deserted alleyway otherwise, it was quiet. The sun was high in the sky by the time I saw a young male with the Junak tattoo on his shoulder. He was indeed carrying a messenger bot down the alley.

Out of the corner of my eye, I saw someone else creeping along the shadows of the alley. A hooded figure weaved around crates and under awnings. They were clearly skilled in the art of stealth. The hooded person stopped moving and glanced up. I quickly moved away from the edge of the roof to avoid being spotted. By the time I looked down the alley again, the person was hiding behind some crates close to a door marked "Kovax Shipping".

The young male, unaware of the danger he was in, approached the door as well. I tensed my muscles, preparing to jump down from my perch at any moment. He reached the door and knocked twice. The person in the shadows inched closer. The door opened, and the male handed off the messenger bot with few words spoken between him and the receiver.

The hooded figure stood and came out from behind the crates. The male looked frozen as if he doesn't know what to do next. The wind flapped the interloper's hood enough to show about half their face, and I'd be damned if they didn't look like Layla.

I jumped from the roof to the ground, only feeling a slight reverberation through my feet. A jump like that would have broken my legs as a human, but as this cat man, my altered feet were more like large paws with reinforced bones that could absorb a fall from almost any height. I stepped closer to Layla and the young man. I could see the bottom half of her face under the hood and her mouth was pulled down in a frown. I could imagine she was none too pleased to see me.

"Now, what do we have here," I asked. The young man, seeing that his would-be attacker was distracted, ran for it, and all Layla could do was watch as he disappeared down the alley. I saw her crouch down as if she was about to sprint. I was faster though. I grabbed her wrist before she could take off, and pinned her arms up above her head against the wall. She glared at me, completely unafraid, and damn but that was hot.

"This is the second time I've caught you somewhere you weren't supposed to be. Now why might that be?" I loosened my grip on her wrists, but just a fraction. There was something about Layla that told me she would be all too happy to take any advantage of me letting my guard down.

"It isn't a crime to walk down an alley," she said through gritted teeth.

"On that account, I agree, but that still begs the question why walk down this specific alley at this exact time of day? I think you were trying to intercept a package that wasn't meant for you, or perhaps you just wanted to question the person who delivered it."

Her face scrunched up in frustration as she tried to wiggle free of my grasp. "Get your hands off me, barbarian." Her voice was deeper than usual. It had a sexy raspiness to it.

"I'll gladly unhand you, sweetheart, as soon as you tell me why you're here." Her look of frustration morphed into a calm, placid look of determination. One minute I was holding a beautiful woman by the wrists, the next my head felt like it had nearly been split open. She'd headbutted me with those damned horns of hers.

I staggered backward, and apparently, my head wound wasn't enough for her. She stalked forward holding a very familiar dagger and stabbed me in the shoulder with it. I leaned against the wall for support and I smiled at the clearly very talented Layla.

"I've been wondering where that went," I chuckled.

Layla's self-satisfied look of victory turned into a frown. She hadn't been expecting that reaction from me. I mean who would? I'd been stabbed and instead of being offended, I was honored that a woman such as her would take the time to pierce me at all.

"Next time I tell you to unhand me and you don't, I'll aim for your heart instead of your shoulder." Her tone was harsh, but her tail was thrashing. My reaction must have really annoyed her.

"I don't doubt it," I chuckled again. She huffed, reached for my dagger, then yanked it free from my shoulder. I winced at the pain but was otherwise unharmed.

"I'm taking this with me," she held up the silver dagger I'd purchased just two weeks ago.

"Consider it a gift, sweetheart!" I yelled to her as she walked away. "You still haven't told me why you were here!" I shouted again.

"And I never will," she yelled back over her shoulder.

"Oh I'll get some answers out of you yet. You can count on that."

Her body disappeared as she left the alley and turned onto the street.

I took a deep breath and started what was going to be a painful walk home. My shoulder had already started to throb and the bleeding didn't look like it was going to stop anytime soon.

I'd known that woman would be trouble, I'd just had no idea exactly how much. But she was the good kind of trouble and I couldn't wait to see what she did next.

* * *

Latisha

Up down around over. Ugh! This blasted stitch was impossible! This was the one task I haven't mastered while working in the Kach mortress. Stitching these napkins with these impossible flowers, just so Kach's guests could soil them with their greedy fingers, felt so stupid to me.

"You're handling those napkins a little aggressively today. Something bothering you, Layla?" Cassia asked as she finished yet another perfectly embroidered cloth napkin.

"Did you ask someone to the ball and they said no?" Bexi jested, laughing at her own joke. "I'm just teasing, Layla. Don't look so sour," she elbowed me. "Any male would be lucky to dance with you."

I took a calming breath and unclenched my hand from the sorry-looking cloth napkin. "No, I've just had a rough afternoon." I must have had an edge in my tone because the females backed away from me slightly.

"Just asking, no need to take it out on me...or the napkins." Cassia looked down at my napkin with a torn look as if she was considering if she should save it from my savagery.

With the softest, most feminine voice I could produce I said, "my apologies. I'll be a little less aggressive with them from now on."

"What happened to you?" I could hear the concern in Rali's voice as she walked toward someone in the hallway.

"I met a pretty lady, but I don't think she's quite warmed up to me yet." I stood frozen in place and held my breath. That was Bowen's voice. I had prepared myself for this. If he outed me I was currently just ten steps away from the side entrance through the kitchen. Why did I have to stab him? I could have just run away; he was already wounded from my headbutt. He was just so aggravating that I couldn't help myself. Why couldn't he be afraid of me just like everyone else?

"A pretty female? Bowen you say the strangest things. If you don't want to tell me what happened just say so." Rali sounded a little less concerned this time.

"It's not a secret. A very pretty woman took the time out of her day to pierce me with one of my own daggers." He was slurring his words a bit, probably from a loss of blood and his long walk home.

"Bowen, really, I don't know what to make of you. Come on, I'll walk you to the medical supply closet and patch you up." I heard them shuffle past the kitchen and continue down the hallway.

"You're too kind, Ms. Rali."

"Yes, I know, but don't tell anyone. I have a reputation to uphold."

"Your secret is safe with me." I listened as their footsteps grew softer and softer until I couldn't hear them anymore. I let out a deep sigh and thanked the goddess for my luck this day. A part of me wished Bowen would have just outed me so I could be rid of him, but it seemed I would have to deal with the barbarian for a little longer.

* * *

Latisha

"Pass the spice shaker down here," Drav called down the table. He was sitting next to Airna who blushed every time their shoulders rubbed. *Ugh, younglings and their young love. Gross.*

"Sure thing." Emed gave the shaker a good push and it slid across the wood to Drav.

Tonight's dinner was another bland vegetable stew. The cook gave his apologies before he sat down to dine, and explained how once again his request to use more seasoning, vegetables, noodles, and just about anything else in the servant's meals was denied. Most of us nodded our heads with understanding and continued eating our bland soup.

"I saw the servant's ball decorations come in today. Everything is going to look so pretty." Airna beamed with excitement.

"The ball is next week already," Bexi added

while doing a little happy dance in her chair.

"I don't know. I'd rather get extra pay and the night off than participate in a ball we have to set up ourselves." Yariletta commented and Bexi elbowed her in the side.

"Would you let me have this? Life is hard enough as it is, so please just give me this one piece of joy."

"Sorry," Yariletta frowned at her soup bowl. "It's just frustrating, is all."

"And what about you, youngling? Are you going to ask a pretty female or a handsome male to the ball?" Venpan ruffled Marza's hair.

"Hey, stop it!" The male youngling on the edge of becoming a young man batted Venpan's hand away and frantically ran his fingers through his hair to fix it.

Once he was satisfied his hair was back in its rightful spot laying in a perfectly shaggy way over his forehead and horns, he looked down into his bowl and whispered, "maybe…"

"Maybe what?" Venpan pressed.

"Maybe I'll ask someone to the ball."

"Are you scared, Marza?" The elder male nudged him with his elbow.

Marza gave him a piercing look before returning to his soup, "No." Venpan laughed, unphased by the youngling's glares.

"We've all been there. You'll regret not asking them much more than you'll regret asking them and getting rejected. Be brave, and just go for it!"

"Here! Here!" Emed cheered and lifted his mug of tea.

Vinee stood on his chair with his mug raised and bellowed, "To the bravery it takes to find love, and to all the brave souls who go after it."

"Here! Here!" Everyone else at the table cheered with mugs raised, including me. Not that I believed in love, but I couldn't be the odd person out.

The conversation at the dinner table died down. Heavy footfalls preceded the Barbarian coming down the steps with his bowl of soup and piece of bread. This must truly be my unlucky day as the only seat left at the table was the one across from mine. He settled in across from me and did a strange eye motion. He kept one eye open while quickly closing and opening the other eyelid. It was probably a threat of some kind. I would have to keep my guard up tonight.

He had a bandage wrapped around his shoulder and moved stiffly instead of with his normal grace.

"What happened to you? Did you fight ten men at once?" Venpan questioned Bowen.

"Oh this? It's just a scratch, one might even call it a flirtation. A beautiful woman plunged a dagger into my shoulder." Bowen had an irritating grin on his face.

"How could that be a flirtation?"

"Because she could have just as easily stabbed me in the heart, but she didn't, so she must care for me in some way." He began eating his dinner as if his stab wound was of little concern to him.

"You sure are a strange one, Bowen," Emed commented.

"I've been called worse." Bowen shrugged his shoulders and winced at the pain. After he took a few more bites of his soup he looked in my direction. The corner of his mouth turned up as if I had just told a funny joke, and I wanted to stab him all over again.

"Speaking of fighting, any news from the Junak?" Venpan asked no one in particular.

"Yeah, when are we going to have our revenge?" Emed chimed in.

Vinee looked around the room and lowered his voice to a very conspiratorial tone. "I'd be ready next week for action. I haven't heard any specifics other than that."

Oh, how I would have liked to have questioned that Sirret male after he dropped off that messenger bot. The odds were good that he would have known something helpful. I looked over at Bowen and my desire to stab him hit me all over again.

CHAPTER 5

Bowen

After dinner concluded, most of the servants headed down to the rec room. I wanted to get up and follow Layla as soon as she parted from the dinner table, but I knew that would only cause more trouble. She was already eyeing me like she wanted to stab me again, and while that might be fun, I think receiving one stab wound a day was my limit.

I waited until everyone left the table before I made my way to the rec room as well. The room was dimly lit just like every other room the servants used, but at least this room was dry, unlike the damp, musty dining room. I'd been told this used to be an old pantry before Monstaire Kach had his new one built.

I'd heard him gloat to his rich friends about his generosity in buying the servants board games and several decks of cards so they could have a place for a little R and R, but the irony of it all was that if he just paid everyone a little more we could all go out to a bar and have some real fun.

"Haha! I win this round!" I looked around the room and saw Layla sitting at a small card table with

Venpan and Vinee. There was a seat open across from Layla, and I found myself suddenly in the mood for a card game.

"So when did the rebellion first reach out to you?" Layla asked Vinee as she casually shuffled the cards.

"Oh, months ago. I was caught stealing some bread on my break, and a group of rebels hid me away in their safe house. I asked to join the rebellion as a way to show my gratitude. They took me up on my offer and said I'd be their main contact in the Dinak house."

"So how do they contact you?" Layla asked as she continued to shuffle.

Vinee gave her a suspicious look. "You don't need to worry about that. I'll keep you updated on all you need to know." He stretched as if he were tired and got up from the table. "I think it's time for me to play a different game." Venpan followed him to the alien equivalent of an air hockey table.

"Those were some interesting questions you were asking," I commented as I sat down across from the sexiest woman in the room.

"Am I not allowed to ask questions?" Layla was shuffling the cards more aggressively now that I had arrived.

"You can ask whatever questions you want. I was just stating the obvious."

Layla set the deck of cards down on the table and walked to the dartboard, tail thrashing behind her.

I followed her and grabbed a set of darts for myself. I could tell she was agitated, and I'd like to move past this awkwardness we had between us, but we wouldn't be able to do that until I got some much-needed answers out of her.

"How would you like to make a wager with me? If I win, you have to tell me why you were in that alleyway today. If you win, well, you can ask or do whatever you'd like to me." My tail thumped on the floor. I'd love to see how creative Layla could get in the bedroom.

"I'd like to stab you again." I'd expected that. She leveled me with a withering glare, and although I knew she was capable of violence, I didn't think she'd stab me again in a room full of onlookers.

I patted my uninjured arm "I've got a good shoulder just waiting to be pierced."

Layla rolled her eyes and moved forward with the conversation, "If I win you have to stop asking me questions."

"Fine by me. You've got yourself a deal." I held out my hand to make it official.

Layla looked at my hand as if it were a snake ready to strike. "What are you doing?"

"Where I come from a deal isn't final until you shake on it," I clarified.

She let out a resigned sigh and shook my hand. "Barbaric." As soon as our hands met I felt a jolt of electricity shoot through my body. It was the first time I didn't feel numb since I'd been altered.

Regaining my composure I gestured to the

dartboard, "Ladies first."

Layla gave me a curt nod and lined up her shot. She threw her dart with an elegant grace and hit the bullseye. Perhaps challenging her to a dart game wasn't the best idea.

"Not bad," I acknowledged, trying to look as calm as possible.

I lined up my dart and shot it toward the board. *Thwack!* I'd gotten a bullseye too.

Layla frowned and grabbed another dart. With a steady hand, she threw the dart forward. It landed just outside of the bullseye.

"Looks like you better start coming up with an answer to your whereabouts this morning." I winked at her and grabbed my next dart.

"You should get your eye checked out. It keeps twitching," she commented.

"It's..." I looked down and tried not to smile. I knew my southern way of speaking threw people off, but there was very little I had left of myself out here and my accent was one of those things. It was just an added bonus that Layla found it so irritating, and god was she cute when she took me so literally. "My eye isn't twitching. I'm winking at you. It's like an acknowledgment of a secret shared between two people."

"Well, stop it. It's strange and it makes you look ill."

"Alright, sweetheart," I conceded as I threw my next dart. It was also a little outside of the bullseye.

"Do they not teach barbarians how to play

darts where you come from?" Layla couldn't hold back her smile at my loss of points as she picked up her next dart.

"As a matter of fact, they do. You'll see, I'll hit the target on my next turn."

"Uh huh..." She threw her next dart and of course, it was another bullseye. *Damn! I'll never get answers out of her if she wins.*

I concentrated and threw my next dart. *Ah hell!* It landed on the ring separating the bullseye from the rest of the board.

"Now that counts." I pointed at the board.

Layla's jaw hung open, flabbergasted that I would even suggest such a thing. "It does not!" *I should have known she wouldn't fall for that.*

"Look, where I come from hitting that little ring around the center target counts as still being a bullseye."

"Well you're not on your barbaric planet anymore, so it doesn't count." She was resolute in her declaration and I knew there'd be no changing her mind. I'd just have to hope for a miracle that she might miss her next shot.

"Fine," I huffed, acting as casual as I could under the circumstances.

"Don't pout Barbarian, not everyone has good aim." She practically purred the words like her voice itself was gloating over my loss.

"Well, I certainly experienced your good aim this morning when you stabbed me." I pointed to my shoulder for effect.

Layla's cheeks flushed a dark blue and her tail thumped the floor once before she grabbed it. She took a deep breath and threw her dart. It also landed outside of the bullseye.

"You distracted me with your chatter. Darts should be a silent game," she pouted.

"Now where would be the fun in that?" I smirked.

❊ ❊ ❊

Latisha

I WILL win this game. I could not stand this stupid male and his stupid handsome face, and I certainly wouldn't lose to him in darts! Once this was over I'd be rid of him forever.

Bowen stood poised to throw his dart as he moved his hand back and forth, getting ready to launch it. I was suddenly struck with a genius idea. I lightly whacked his butt with my tail just as he threw the dart, and he nearly missed the board entirely. *Yes!* I inwardly rejoiced and tried not to think about how nicely my tail had bounced off his very firm ass.

He turned to me and looked me squarely in the eyes, but before he could speak I said, "You really need to practice your aim."

He crossed his arms over his broad chest and raised an eyebrow at me. "I never took you for a cheater."

"What, am I not allowed to move my tail now?"

I pretended to be annoyed.

"You can move your tail all you want, but if you want to smack my ass with it I know a private room we can go to fulfill all your ass-smacking dreams." My heart skipped a beat at his words. Why did the idea of that sound so nice? Ugh! This awful male and his strange human ways.

"I have no desire to touch you. That handshake is the last bit of contact you can expect from me." I crossed my arms over my chest and gave him a defiant look.

He took a step forward and leaned down to speak in my ear. I caught a whiff of his scent. It was a nice mix of musky woods and spices.

"You better stop being mean to me, Layla or I'm going to fall in love with you." My heart was suddenly stuck in my throat. I'd given this male every reason to hate me, and yet he dared to draw closer. There was a vulnerability in being liked by someone who had seen you at your worst. I didn't like it; to be vulnerable was to be weak. *Don't trust anyone.* My mother's words rang through my head. I backed away from Bowen and grabbed the second to last dart.

"Last one, better make it count," he smirked.

I swallowed the lump in my throat and tried not to think about how Bowen's scent was still tickling my nose. I took a deep breath, aimed, and threw. Bullseye.

"Damn," Bowen muttered under his breath. It was nice to know he was disappointed. My victory would be all the sweeter for it.

"No cheatin' this time." He did a strange gesture where he pointed two fingers at his eyes and then pointed them back at me. From the context I could assume he meant he was watching me. I held my tail in my hands to indicate I would not be touching him with it again. He threw his last dart and it landed right outside the bullseye.

I could not contain the grin that spread across my face. "I will finally enjoy some peace now that you won't be pestering me with questions."

"Don't get too comfortable, I'm going to ask for a rematch soon." His ears twitched in a curious way. He may have better control over his tail than I did, but his twitching ears were giving away how irritated he really felt.

"Be sure to practice, I prefer to play against a skilled opponent." I did his silly eye twitch that he called a wink and walked away.

CHAPTER 6

Latisha

"It's so nice to see you, Kach. It's been so long," Dirgach greeted my boss.

I was dusting the high shelves and tall lamps in the entryway of the Dirgach house when Kach walked in. I had stolen a maroon apron worn by the Dirgach house staff from their laundry room and stationed myself as close to the house entrance as I could. Kach had spoken about taking a meeting today at house Dirgach, and I'd needed to be here to listen in on their conversation.

"Too long if you ask me." Kach sounded very confident for a male in enemy territory. What was he doing here? How could a meeting with Dirgach benefit him? Of all the rival houses Dirgach was by far the least trustworthy.

"Come, let's retire to the study for a more private conversation." *I'll have to find another way to listen in.* I made my way down one floor and deftly avoided the gaze of any house servants I passed. I found a closet that was located directly under the study and stood on a stool to put my ear to the air vent.

"And that is my proposal." Dirgach's voice sounded muffled, but I could still understand what he was saying. Biff me, I wasted too much time finding this room. I had no idea what proposal they were talking about.

"How do I know I can trust you? It was just last year that I stole a business deal from you. How do I know you aren't just trying to retaliate?" Now Kach sounded nervous. I would be too if I were him.

"Oh, that's old news. There are no hard feelings. It was just business, right?" Now it was Dirgach who was sounding confident; too confident. If I was Kach I wouldn't trust a word coming out of his mouth.

"Right." Kach's tone sounded dubious.

"Shall we meet next week to discuss this further? I'll be happy to host you again."

My attention was pulled away from the conversation in the study by voices and footsteps approaching the closet.

"I'm telling you it's in this closet, not the one upstairs." Bif me! The servants were headed right this way. I scrambled down from the stool and left the closet as quickly as I could, holding multiple dusters over my face.

Halfway down the hallway, I ditched the duster tools and headed for the ground-level exit. I was so busy looking behind me that I ran right into a muscled furry chest carrying the scent of musky woods and spices.

Goodness no. I looked up into piercing green eyes, Bowen's eyes. His brows were furrowed together in a confused expression.

I heard more people approaching and looked over Bowen's shoulder to see both Monstair Kach and Dirgach coming this way.

Bowen turned around and tucked me behind him. "Monstair Kach, I suggest you use the north exit. This hallway was just mopped and it looks rather treacherous."

"I don't remember asking the servants to mop today. Ah well, come with me, we'll head to the other exit," Dirgach sighed.

Bowen turned back around and pinned me with a pointed glare. "You know, sweetheart, the first few times were fun, but now you're beginning to be a professional pain in my ass."

"I touched your ass *one* time, I am in no way a professional at it." The audacity of this male would never cease to amaze me. I should be grateful that he saved me from being caught by Kach, but I just couldn't find it within myself, he was just *so* irritating. It was especially irritated by the cute way his ears twitched when he was agitated and the way his soft skin felt when I shook his hand, not to mention his tight ass that I found myself looking at way too often. Everything about this male was insufferable.

Bowen's face softened. "You're cute when you take everything I say so literally."

"I am not cute!"

"As they say, the eye of the beholder and all that. What I mean is I don't like running into you like this." The corner of his mouth turned up in a wicked grin. "You know, if you want to see me more often all you have to do is ask. You don't have to sneak around another mortress to get my attention."

"I am not here to see you!" I whisper-shouted.

"Then why are you here?" Bowen raised an eyebrow at me.

I snapped my jaw shut. "I have a friend who works here. She needed the day off, and I told her I'd cover for her."

"How generous of you. What's your friend's name?" He crossed his arms over his chest and tapped a finger on his bicep as he waited for my answer. *Bif me, what's a common name?*

"Kayla! Her name is Kayla."

Just then a servant walked by and Bowen grabbed him by the arm. "Tell me, does a Kayla work here?"

The servant's eyebrows furrowed in confusion. "No. I've never heard of a Kayla working here."

Bowen let go of the male's arm. "Thank you for your time."

We were standing next to the wall and when Bowen turned around he placed a hand on either side of my head and leaned in with a very serious look.

"Layla, I'm going to need you to stop blowing smoke up my ass, and give me some real answers."

"You make a lot of references to your ass for someone whose butt is as flat as a dinner plate." That was a lie. His ass was most certainly not flat and I knew that all too well from staring at it so much.

He leaned in even closer. "What did I tell you

about being mean to me?" His usually composed tail was thumping the floor.

My heart started to race and even though Bowen was already so close to me I wanted him even closer. *No. I can't want that.* I had a multitude of reasons why I couldn't want that. I crossed my arms and looked down at the floor.

"What, cat got your tongue?"

"Do you have a single phrase that doesn't involve a body part, Barbarian?"

"Probably not. Now tell me why you were in Kach's room the other day, then in the alleyway, and now here of all places?" He impatiently tapped his foot.

"I won our bet last night which means I don't have to answer any of your questions." I ducked under his arm and started to walk away. He was in front of me in a flash. How he had such speed I had no idea.

"You're right. I did agree to not ask you any more questions. So how about this, I'm going to make some statements and you're going to nod your head if they're true and shake your head if they're not."

I crossed my arms and impatiently tapped my own foot this time. "And why would I do that?"

"Because if I'm going to keep saving your tight blue ass, I'd like to know what I'm saving you from and why." So he'd admired my ass as well? I'd file that information away for later.

"I never asked you to save me," I huffed. I was genuinely embarrassed that he'd had to save me on a few occasions now; grateful, but embarrassed.

"No you didn't, but I've had to cover for you all the same, and at the rate you're going I'm going to be saving you again tomorrow."

He pinched the bridge of his nose and sighed. "First statement. You're a woman of many skills and very few of them involve servant's work."

I slowly nodded my head. There wasn't much harm in confirming that I had skills that went beyond serving, dusting, and making beds.

"Ok. Second statement. You asked very pointed questions of the other servants, as if you were conducting an investigation." *Am I that obvious?* I didn't make a move. I wasn't confirming that.

"Well?" He continued to stand in front of me like a soft, furry wall of muscle.

"I think I should be going." I attempted to walk past him, but he grabbed my arm.

"I'll take that as a yes." There was a long pause before he continued again. "You're working for someone other than Kach."

"Let go of me." I grunted, and I was surprised when he immediately did. I'd expected him to hold me hostage until he finished interrogating me. Maybe he did learn his lesson when I stabbed his shoulder.

"I'll take that as another yes. You're working for the rebellion." I couldn't help but smirk. Finally, he'd gotten something wrong.

"Hmm interesting, judging by your smile I'll assume I'm wrong on that one." Immediately my face fell into a frown.

A large group of servants walked down the

hallway and I took the opportunity to step away from Bowen. I wedged myself in the middle of the group and looked back to see a frustrated Bowen with his twitching ears standing alone in the middle of the corridor. I knew I'd have to face him again at the Kach mortress, but by then I'd have a better plan to avoid his questions.

* * *

Bowen

I'm on to you Layla. She wasn't a regular servant. I doubt she was a servant at all, and she's obviously interested in knowing more about the rebellion, but why? Who was she really working for?

My expression must have given away the fact that I was in a foul mood because when I passed the other guards at Kach's house they all felt the need to comment on it.

"What's wrong, catman? Did you have a rough day cleaning your fur?" Gunok wasn't the sharpest knife in the drawer, and he was certainly not original with his insults.

"No, I did actual work, unlike you fellas," I spouted off.

"You hear that? The mutant thinks he's better than us." Cruun pounded a fist into his open palm as a threat. Not that he could ever catch me, slow lumbering fool that he was.

This was why I never dined with the guards. Technically they were higher class than the servants, and they were all too happy to remind everyone of that, but they gave off big ACAB vibes if you asked me.

I've never been a big fan of the cops. The only time I saw them as a kid was when they were busting my papaw's moonshine operation. Then when I grew up all my high school bullies became police officers and that's all I needed to know about the kind of people the police force attracted. They're all small men with big egos desperate to gain any scrap of power they can.

The guards here are the same. They got a little bit of power and it all went to their heads. They didn't realize that just like the servants they were scrambling to catch the crumbs that fell off the master's table. In a system that only benefited the rich, we were all oppressed.

I made it to my post on the roof and sat on my haunches watching every passerby below. Men, women, and children: they were all the same. I felt nothing when I saw them and I felt nothing when I interacted with them...that was except for Layla. Speaking with her, taunting her, touching her—everything about her was like a bolt of lightning straight into my veins.

Being fucked with by those scientists had left me feeling like I was on a high dose of an antidepressant that suppressed all my emotions. I felt nothing about anything, and I thought I'd feel that way for the rest of my life, but Layla was like a fire in the darkness, the spark of life I never expected to find again. Even if she didn't make me feel alive I would still be infatuated with her all the same. She was clever, talented, didn't take shit from anyone, and had a body that my hands ached to touch.

I didn't think she was looking for a mate, and truth be told, I wasn't either. I was broken in more ways than one. But that didn't mean I was going to stop pestering her and saving her until the day I died. She was a closed-off person and she must have her reasons for keeping everyone at arm's length. I wouldn't push her into a relationship she didn't want, but maybe after a while, she'd accept me as a friend.

Hell, there were worse things in life than to banter with and be insulted by the prettiest woman in the Feno Galaxy.

CHAPTER 7

Latisha

I laid down in bed and tried not to think about how I ran into Bowen again today. If he hadn't looked so surprised to see me, I'd have thought he'd implanted a tracker on me somehow. *At this rate, I'm going to be saving you again tomorrow.* I replayed his words in my head. He wouldn't ever save me again. I was going to make sure of that.

The door to our dorm creaked open and someone softly walked to the bed next to mine.

"Good evening Bexi, I received your message to join you tonight." The male whispered. It was Emed.

"Hurry under the covers before anyone sees you," Bexi whispered. He did as he was told, and the once quiet room was now filled with whispered giggles and quiet laughter. The giggles quickly turned into moans, and I sighed as I put my pillow over my head to muffle the sound.

How nice for them. I didn't even say the words out loud and they still sounded bitter in my head. All of my sexual experiences had been less than great. Of the few times I'd been with a male, it was during a rut.

I wasn't sexually attracted to females or I would have attempted to rut with one long ago. As an allgender, I got one rut once every six months like a male, but it only lasted for one day like a female.

It'd been a few years since I'd had the courage to go to a rut specialist for assistance. The last Sirret male I met with was nice enough, but as soon as I took off my clothes his face scrunched up in disgust. Sirret women didn't have any external pleasure points as everything was contained within the slit of their sex; however, as an allgender I had both internal gonads and a small nub over my slit. When an intersex woman grew an external pleasure point, no matter how big or small, the medical community called it a perilla, and my perilla was what turned most males off when they saw my body. It was an imperfection in their eyes, and our society demanded flawless beauty. I also didn't have a womb but I'd never been interested in having children so that didn't bother me.

Despite all the social hardship my body had caused me I couldn't say that I hated it. I went to a medic-recommended affinity group for allgeners once. Many of them struggled with unbalanced hormones that caused them to grow more hair than a non-allgender would, and some adults were dealing with facial blemishes that usually only plagued adolescents.

I was pleased that despite the fact that my virile glands didn't produce male hormones as one usually should, my internal gonads did produce them which left me mostly balanced in the end.

My voice may have been deeper than most females, but I liked the raspiness of it. I knew I was supposed to hate my body, but I didn't. It was me, and I liked myself: broken horns, perilla, and all.

The moaning in the bed next to mine was still going on and I tried to block it out. Especially Bexi's moans.

I couldn't say I've derived much pleasure from sex. The males I'd mated with outside of the rut specialists always made me face away from them, while they painfully tugged my tail out of the way and then shuttled into me so hard and fast I didn't even have a moment to settle into the sensations. As soon as they reached their climax they would leave and ask if I could just finish myself off. I always said I could, which was true, but that wasn't what I was there for. I wanted a slow sexual experience with a stranger I could have a one-night stand with and never think about again.

Don't trust anyone would always run through my head every time I started to become attached to someone. I couldn't afford to actually fall in love with or trust anyone. But that didn't mean I didn't want to enjoy myself.

I'd mostly given up on the idea of taking another mating partner. It was always going to be the same sad experience, and I'd had enough of those already.

* * *

Latisha

At breakfast the next day, I grabbed a piece of bread and put some jam on top of it.

"Aren't you going to sit down and eat?" Yariletta asked as she grabbed a plate.

"No, I've got an errand to run." In truth, I'd rather die than eat across from Bowen today. I avoided him last night because he was on duty, but I didn't think I'd be so lucky today. He'd gotten too close to the truth behind why I was here, and it would be best if I avoided him in the future.

I entered the kitchen and spied a basket full of yesterday's unused root vegetables.

"Good morning Rali, do you have plans for that basket of leftover food?" I pointed to the container on the floor.

Rali looked up from the bread she was kneading and saw the basket. "I can't say that I do. Did you want to take it off my hands?"

"Yes, I'd love to." I gave Rali a polite nod and headed out the door. As soon as the morning sun hit my face I sighed a deep breath of relief. It was nice to be out of the mortress. It was also nice to put some distance between myself and Bowen.

I headed for a safe house that was known to hold some of the displaced families that had lost their only shelter after the warehouse fire. They were sympathetic to the rebellion's cause and they might have some information that the servants at Kach's house didn't.

As I walked down the street I passed the Vorsts Drannon had described in his report. Heron, Cro, and Albi. Heron was working on a broken hover cart and was pointing things out to the other Vorsts.

Not too far down from them, I saw females and children playing on the stoop of the safe house.

"Good morning," I greeted them all, careful not to step on any of the toys scattered around. "A friend sent me to deliver this." I handed a female in a red dress the basket of leftover food.

Her eyes grew wide with surprise. "Oh, thank you, thank you very much. Who sent you?" The woman took the basket and gave a deep bow of gratitude.

"The person who gifted the basket wants to remain anonymous, but they want you to know the rebellion is strong and growing stronger." None of that was true of course. I had no real way of knowing if the rebellion was growing stronger. I just hoped it would encourage the female to give me whatever information she knew.

The female sitting next to her leaned in and whispered, "Rumor is there's something happening next week."

The female in the red dress added, "I heard they're taking down a merchant house." That was a bigger retaliation than I'd expected.

"Oh wow, that's a big move," I commented.

"It's about time. They won't listen to us unless we do something drastic. It's time to make our move," the woman wearing the red dress added.

"How have you been since the fire?" I had been genuinely concerned for the rebels who had been in the warehouse that night. From what Drannon had described it was pretty horrific.

The women looked at each other. The one sitting on the porch sighed. "Things are ok. A few of us have found work and our mates were hired on to that secret construction project. It's hard not knowing when they'll be back."

"Have you gotten any word on what they've been doing?" Toran has been able to communicate a few messages to the team via his transmitter necklace, but so far it was nothing interesting. One-half of the workers were building a tall structure aboveground while he and the other half of the workers were building a structure underground.

"No, no word. They don't allow buzzpads or any other devices on the worksite, and they have to sleep in tents on the site until the job is done."

Two rough-looking Sirret men were walking down the street, and something about them made me uneasy. I kept an eye on their movements but otherwise paid attention to the conversation in front of me.

The woman in the dress sighed. "They really don't want anyone to know what they are working on."

"Cycle after cycle without hearing a word from them is awful," The other woman added.

Hmm, another dead end. At least I'd learned the rebellion was going to mount a big attack soon.

Maybe the Junak would show up and take off his mask. That would make my job a lot easier.

The two men who had been walking up the street now stood a few feet away from the stoop.

"What have we here?" the tall man with an orange jacket asked as he stood uncomfortably close to me.

"It looks like a bunch of females who need work," the skinny man commented.

"Why don't we go inside and I can pay you for some very specific services?" Orange jacket with his hot breath said as he slid his tail up and down my leg.

"Poor male has been kicked out of every rut specialist resort on Ozinda and Varis 2." Skinny laughed as if being marked as a bad client was somehow a mark of pride instead of a bad omen.

"Hey! It's not my fault their specialists can't take a few hits along with a few rough thrusts." Orange jacket put his hands on his hips and did a few mock thrusts to demonstrate. Skinny adjusted himself as if he were enjoying the show.

Orange jacket took another step closer to me, but I held my hand palm out to his shoulder and stopped him from coming any closer.

"You don't want to do that," I warned. I palmed the dagger I kept hidden in my apron pocket. Out of the corner of my eye, I spotted the Vorsts walking toward us. Each of them palmed knives of their own, ready to jump in at a moment's notice.

* * *

Bowen

"How much for this red fruit here?" I asked the produce stand vendor.

"Three credits."

"Three credits for one piece of fruit?" I couldn't believe what I was hearing.

The man shrugged and said, "It's a good fruit."

"I'll tell you–" My sentence died in my throat as my very sensitive ears heard some men bragging about being kicked out of some brothels. "I'll be back." I put down the fruit and headed toward the ruckus.

I turned the corner to leave the market and saw two men hassling a group of women sitting outside their house. One of the women was standing with her back to me. Her scent caught on the breeze and there was something familiar about it. Unfortunately, it was mixed with the vile unwashed scents of the two men near her as well.

"Hey! It's not my fault their specialists can't take a few hits along with a few rough thrusts." A Sirret man in an orange jacket thrust his hips out like a middle school boy acting well below his raising. The jacketed man took another step toward the lady who was standing and she quickly put out her hand to stop him from coming any closer. The movement caused her to turn to the side and I could tell from her side profile that the woman was Layla. Something feral snapped inside of me, like an emotion had finally been cut loose inside my gut and I was feeling the full force of a year's worth of anger all at once.

A few Vorst's stopped what they were doing and slowly walked up to the men. Their actions were commendable to be sure, but I would take it from here. I held some clout as a personal bodyguard to a merchant and today I intended on using it.

The man put his hand on Layla's wrist to move it out of the way, and I swore my heart had never beat faster in my life. In no time at all I was toe-to-toe with the man. Without wasting a minute I pulled back my arm and launched my fist at his jaw. I heard a small crack and a *whomp* as the man fell flat on his ass.

The man left standing had a startled expression on his face. "We didn't start any trouble with you. What was that for?"

I pointed directly at Layla whose eyes were as wide as saucers at my unexpected visit and I made myself clear. "Her trouble is my trouble."

"You looking for a fight, cat freak?" The jacketed man stood back up on his feet and held up his fists.

"I'll have it out with you, if that's what you require." I put my fists up in the air as well. I'd been skinny most of my life. I learned at a very young age that I couldn't take a punch, but I sure could dodge one.

"It isn't enough that you look weird, you have to talk weird, too?" The man laughed at his own joke.

Blessedly, the big man did not waste any more time with jests and lunged at me with all the grace of a fat cat on a hot day. I easily dodged his jab and his right hook, too. I squatted to the ground with one leg sticking out and swept my leg under both of his. The man fell down with a thump and Mr. Skinny joined the brawl.

He landed one good punch to my ribs before I dodged out of the way. But this man was in the mood to fight dirty. I'd heard that Sirrets counted tail pulling as off limits in a fight, so I was surprised when I felt a sharp pain at the base of my spine from my tail being harshly pulled to the side.

Two could play that game. Growing up poor and skinny made me an easy target for bullies, and I quickly learned how to fight someone on their level. No matter my feelings on fighting dirty, if my opponent fought dirty, I fought dirty. It was what I had to do to survive.

I spun around, ignoring the pain that was now radiating up my spine, and pulled out a knife, grabbed his tail, and sliced the end off.

A piercing screech filled the street. The man held the bleeding end of his tail, and picked the tufted end up off the ground.

The jacketed man got up, ready for more. "Are you biffing crazy?! You don't just slice another male's tail off."

I wiped the blood off my blade with a spare handkerchief and answered the brute. "I do whatever I please, and it pleases me greatly to fight dirty, in fact, I'm quite good at it." I pointed my knife in his direction and asked, "Would you like to lose your tail as well?"

The man had the good sense to look scared, but

then his dumbass looked around at the crowd that surrounded us and puffed out his chest. I knew his type. He was not going to stop until his body gave out. This was a point of pride for him, and currently, his pride had been more grievously wounded than his body.

The brute charged right for me. I shifted out of the way of his punch then grabbed him in a chokehold. He got one good punch to my ribs in before I raked my claws down his back, spilling blood down his blue skin and onto the ground.

I held him up before he could pass out from the blood loss and whispered in his ear, "I should thank you. I've felt dead inside for months, but standing here in the street fighting with you, feeling your last few breaths rustling my fur before you pass out, it's the second time I've felt alive in months. The other time was when I touched that woman, the very woman you just threatened to force yourself upon. Now tell me, are you ever going to threaten her again?"

"No," the man rasped.

"Are you going to come after me when you've healed?" He was already starting to lose consciousness, so I shook him awake.

"Na-no," he breathed.

"Good." I finally let him go and watched as he slumped to the ground.

Everyone around me had a look of shock on their faces.

I stepped over the passed-out man and held my

hand out to Layla, "May I escort you back home? The streets are awful dangerous today."

She hesitated at first and eyed me curiously. She wasn't afraid of me. I would have scented that immediately. Instead, she looked me up and down as if she were seeing me for the first time, and there was a look of admiration on her face.

She eventually reached out her hand and placed it in mine. The same jolt of electricity coursed through me as when our hands first touched. Her hand was tough and calloused just like her, and I was honored to hold it.

CHAPTER 8

Latisha

That was something... Other than the guys on the security team, I'd never had anyone fight for me before. It was an odd feeling. Bowen was a little unhinged, but seeing as it was in my defense it was kind of sexy; a bit intense, but still sexy.

It was a nice change of pace walking with Bowen instead of running from him. His calloused hand reminded me a lot of my own. There was a sense of security in that, that we might be more similar than different. I was emotionally broken and untrusting and he was a little crazy and intense.

I still didn't trust him, of course, but I did feel confident he wouldn't hurt me intentionally, at least not right now. People's motivations could always change.

"You know I could have handled that myself." I couldn't let him get away with thinking I *needed* his help. I had appreciated his help on multiple occasions now, but I'd never *needed* it.

"I don't doubt it. You're a very skilled woman who doesn't hesitate to strike when you need to. I've learned that first hand." He looked down at me with a grin, and I couldn't help but smile at the memory of stabbing him in the shoulder just a few days ago. He seemed to have healed already. The guards had access to quick healing meds which would explain why he was already back in top shape.

"Then why didn't you let me take care of those guys on my own?" I turned my lip down in a pout, but, in truth, I enjoyed having someone stand up for me. It was such a rare occasion that I still couldn't wrap my head around it.

"Well, sweetheart, where I come from a man takes a sense of pride in taking care of a woman, whether it's holding a door open, paying for dinner, or taking out a bully who is eyeing her like a piece of meat for the taking."

The thought of Bowen taking care of me had made my stomach do flip-flops.

"You sure are strange, Barbarian." I needed to agitate him again so he didn't get the wrong idea about us or what we could be.

"In a galaxy full of aliens, I'd rather be strange but still myself than fit in and lose all that I am." His gaze went unfocused as if he were remembering how much had been taken from him already. I understood that part of him, too. I knew what it was like to be physically altered against your will, but he seemed to thrive in his new body just like I thrived in mine.

* * *

Latisha

Dinner that night went about the same as it had since I was hired: there was talk of the rebellion that led nowhere, and talk of the servant's ball that everyone had mixed feelings about. After dinner, most of us went to the rec room. I sat down at the card table with Vinee and Venpan. Vinee always seemed to know what was happening with the rebellion before anyone else did.

Bowen sat down next to me. "May I join you fine folks this evening?"

"Go ahead, your credits are as good as anyone else's and I plan on winning them all." Venpan had a wide grin on his face, full of a gambler's hope.

"We'll see about that, Venpan," Vinee huffed.

Venpan dealt the cards, and I schooled my face into a blank expression. No matter what I was dealt I didn't want to give anything away. The cards I received weren't very good. I let the corner of my mouth turn up ever so slightly to make it seem like I was pleased with what I was given.

"Layla, I never did ask you where you're from. I'd never seen you on this side of town before you started working here," Venpan commented as he shuffled his cards around in his hand.

"I'm from the Osu district." I gave the same cover story that I always did. A little bit of truth mixed with some small lies to make it all sound believable. I wasn't from Osu, but I had spent a lot of time there stealing food to survive when I was a youngling.

"Osu, huh? I guess that's far enough away for us not to have crossed paths before." Venpan concentrated on his cards once again and laid down a set of high numbers for Bowen to match. Up until this point I hadn't been able to tell if Bowen was bluffing or not. His face was completely placid, not giving away a hint of emotion. Now would be the moment of truth.

"You almost got me there friend, but I can match your cards and even do slightly better." He laid down a set of cards that were indeed a better hand than what Venpan had laid out. Now it was Vinee's turn.

As he decided whether or not to play a hand or quit the game, I studied Bowen again. He had only smiled for a moment when he laid his cards down. His face was back to its placid expression now. I wondered if I could throw him off kilter again like I did when I smacked his butt. It had been fun seeing him so flustered and I was eager to see him flustered again. I slowly dragged my tail over his lap. Bowen's eyes went wide and he nearly jumped out of his seat.

"Sorry, I can't control it," I said in a very matter-of-fact tone.

Bowen narrowed his eyes and grabbed the end of my tail right before it could leave his lap entirely. He gently pulled my tail back onto his lap and started stroking it. His fingers teased my skin as they lightly glided up and down my sensitive appendage. His touch sent a shiver down my spine and made my sex throb.

Vinee cleared his throat, "I'm out." He placed

his cards on the table and stomped off. I snatched my tail back from Bowen's lap and tried to focus on my cards. It was difficult given I could still feel Bowen's touch on my skin like a ghost of pleasure just lingering there, promising more to come if I would just reach out and take it.

I put down my three highest cards, ten of hearts, eight of batons, and ten of credits. I only had one card left for the next round, the goddess of hearts. I hoped it would be enough.

"Well, I think that's the end of the line for me." Vepan set his cards down and left the table.

"I guess that just leaves the two of us," Bowen smiled a wicked feline grin.

"I guess so. What do you have?" I gave him a grin that matched his own. Maybe if he thought I had a high card he would just give up. The goddess of hearts wasn't bad, but it wasn't great either.

"Seeing as we both just have one card left why don't we lay them down at the same time?" He waved his one remaining card in the air.

"Why not," I agreed.

"Alright, I'll count us down; three, two, one."

We both laid our cards down; the goddess of hearts and the fool. "Well, would you look at that? We've got a goddess and a fool. Sounds about right wouldn't you say?" He did his annoying eye twitch again.

"I have no idea what you're talking about." I picked up all the cards and stacked them neatly on the table. I knew exactly what he was talking about. He was flirting and calling me a goddess. I would like to be his goddess and he my fool. *No! None of that.* My tail thumped angrily on the floor. I would never be able to trust him enough for that. I couldn't trust anybody.

"Good night, Bowen." I hastily got up from the table and left the room.

CHAPTER 9

Bowen
CW: implied attempted sexual assault

"Why don't you take a twenty-minute break, Bowen? You've earned it." Kach gave me a hard slap on the shoulder as he left his bedroom suite. I could scent his rut was coming. Sirret male rutting pheromones were awful. They were a cloying musky scent and once I smelled it, I couldn't get the stench out of my nose. I understood why I'd never seen a Katsuro on Ozinda before. If I had a choice I wouldn't live on this planet either. The female's rutting scent was a bit lighter and slightly sweet, but overall still unpleasant.

"Thank you Monstair Kach, I'll circle back in twenty minutes." I bowed low and left my master who pretended to be my boss.

I was about to leave the hallway when I heard a distinctly feminine scream. I turned around to see what had happened, but my vision was blocked by a large house plant. On silent feet, I walked back to Kach's room and hid behind the large plant to see what was going on. I caught a glimpse of a servant woman's dress entering the room and the door closing behind her.

This didn't feel right. I may not be a learned man, but I could put two and two together. Kach asked me to leave, I heard a woman scream and now the two of them were behind a locked door.

I walked back to the bedroom suite and typed in the entry code; just as I suspected, it didn't work. This might bite me in this ass later, but I went ahead and pressed the emergency call button. A moment passed and then I heard loud footsteps barreling toward the door. Kach opened it, holding up his unbuttoned trousers.

"What is it?" he growled.

I glanced over Kach's shoulder and saw the young Airna looking very scared on Kach's bed.

"I'm very sorry for the interruption, Monstair Kach, but there's been a bomb threat from a rival house. I'm going to have to ask you to make your way to the bunker."

Kach raked a hand through his hair. "Fine!" He buttoned up his pants and turned to Airna. "You! Call the rut resort and have them send over a specialist tonight. Tell them I'll pay extra for her to come here, and to keep it secret. I'm not attending one of those biffing rutting dinners."

That was rich coming from the guy who'd just hosted one of those dinners and enjoyed it thoroughly as his guests suffered.

"Yes Monstair Kach, right away." Airna rushed to Kach's holocom on the other end of his bedroom suite.

"This better be a real threat. Unless the threat of imminent death is looming over my head I don't want to be disturbed," Kach threatened as he walked down the hallway.

"Of course, Monstair. Once you're safely in the bunker I'll investigate further."

"You do that."

I left the very grumpy Kach to make his way down the bunker while I went back and checked on Airna. "Good afternoon, did you make that holo call?"

"Ye-yes," she stammered, still looking skittish from whatever had happened in here earlier. "The specialist is on her way. She'll be here in ten minutes."

"Well, then I believe you're free to go, Ms. Airna." I pressed the button to open the door.

"Right," she nodded and walked out.

I checked my buzzpad. *Ten minutes, I better head to the gate to warn the rut specialist what she's in for.* I rushed down the stairs and outside to the garage, where I knew I'd find Drav.

"Hey, you might want to check on Airna, she's had a rough afternoon and could use a compassionate shoulder to cry on."

Drav stopped waxing Kach's volt-car and gave me his full attention. It wasn't exactly a secret that Drav and Airna were sweet on each other.

"What happened?" He hurriedly put his supplies away.

"Let's just say a certain Monstair is having his rut and pulled the first available female servant into his chambers." I tried to put it lightly.

CRYSTAL ROSE

"He *what?*" Drav shouted and balled up his fists.

"Now, calm down. I handled it. She didn't come to no harm. Now, you're going to go inside, find Airna, and give her the long firm hug she deserves."

Some of the tension left Drav's shoulders, "Thanks Bowen, I owe you one."

"Don't worry about it. Thwarting Kach's plan and seeing the frustration on his face is enough for me." I left the garage and made my way to the front gate right as an avion woman turned to walk toward the house.

"Hello ma'am, I'm Bowen, Monstair Kach's personal bodyguard. Are you here to see Monstair Kach?" I stepped in front of her, blocking the path.

"Umm yes, I'm Braley, I received a phone call a few minutes ago to come right away." She looked annoyed that I was blocking her way.

"Good, good. Let me show you to his room." We started to walk toward the house as I continued. "Now, I'm afraid Monstair Kach is rather agitated this afternoon, and I don't think he's fixin' to be none too gentle. Is that alright with you or should I ask around for someone else?"

Braley's beak opened slightly in an avion smile. "Oh aren't you the sweetest feline I've ever seen," she patted my chest and continued to walk forward. "I have a corset that protects me like armor and legs that can't be bruised or broken. As for the rest of me, I tend to like it a little rough."

"That's good to hear." And it was. I was relieved to know that she had come prepared. I walked Ms.

Braley up to Kach's room and told her the Monstair would be there soon.

Now for the fun part. I opened the door to the bunker and found Kach pacing back and forth like a caged animal.

"I'm terribly sorry for the inconvenience Monstair Kach. It turns out the bomb threat was a false alarm. One can never be too sure about these things," I apologized.

Kach opened his mouth, undoubtedly to tell me what I could do with my apologies when I cut him off. "But you'll be happy to know that you have a pretty little rut specialist waiting for you in your room as we speak."

The anger on his face dissipated with the good news. "Thank you, Bowen," he sighed. "Might I suggest you be a little less skittish about the next bomb threat?"

"Of course, Monstair Kach, you're absolutely right." I agreed as Kach left the bunker and headed for his personal use house elevator. By the smell in the room, his rut was fully upon him, and I was sure he didn't want to waste any time getting to the rut specialist to relieve himself of that pain.

I leaned back against the wall and let out a deep sigh. That was a close one. In the past, if I had put my neck out for one of the servants like that, I wouldn't have cared what happened to me, but now, all I could think about was Layla and her wicked tail and lovely insults. I actually had something to live for and that was both exhilarating and terrifying. I had a reason to stay on Ozinda, and I knew despite how much I wanted it, I wouldn't leave here without her.

CHAPTER 10

Latisha

"Today's the day!" Bexi giggled as we finished setting up a flower garland that would flow down the banister of the grand staircase. We moved to one of the small side tables at the base of the stairs and filled the large vase with flowers. Yariletta joined us and added some small purple flowers.

"Isn't it exciting? In a few hours we'll be dancing at the ball." Bexi tried to coax a smile out of her friend.

"I don't know, setting up our own ball just to tear it all down tomorrow kind of defeats the purpose," Yariletta shrugged.

"Yari," Bexi nudged her friend with her elbow. "Let Layla enjoy her first ball here."

"I'm with Yariletta on this one," I chimed in. "I'd enjoy the ball a lot more if someone else were setting it up."

"You two are impossible," Bexi huffed as she shoved her next flower into the vase a little too forcefully.

"The dresses and jumpsuits are here!" Rali

yelled from the main entrance. She was standing next to three hover carts all brimming with elegant garments.

A man with a very frilly collared shirt also stood next to the carts. "Alright females of House Dinak, gather around." He followed his statement by clapping his hands twice as if we were cattle to be beckoned. I looked over at Yariletta and saw her rolling her eyes. I would have rolled mine too, but I was genuinely excited about the dresses. It'd been so long since I'd gotten to dress up for anything, and maybe I could use my sex appeal to my advantage.

The female servants of the house all gathered around the carts. The room buzzed with excitement as everyone rifled through the garments, searching for the perfect one.

"Pick one to two pieces to try on, then bring back the one you don't want. Remember these are rentals and you will be charged if you get wine or food on them." The frilly shirt man commented. He must have been the owner of the rental store. I don't think a mere employee would be so snooty.

I made my way to the least crowded box and shifted through the dresses and jumpsuits until I found one that suited me. I lifted out a black dress with a cowl neck, thin straps, and a slit that went up to the thigh. Off to the side was an assortment of shoes we could borrow as well. I grabbed a pair of black high-heeled shoes with thin ankle straps that matched the dress.

A group of us walked upstairs to the bedroom

LUNAR CHAOS

and tried on our garments. I saw the females carrying a variety of dresses from poofy ball gowns, fancy jumpsuits, suits that were tailored to accommodate a female's chest, and tight corsetted dresses that flared at the hips.

We made it to our quarters and everyone stripped, eager to get their outfits on. I turned to the wall as I pulled off my apron and smock. I knew no one would be looking at me as I undressed, and even if they did they wouldn't see anything strange about my body through my underwear, but as an allgender I could never be too careful.

Once fully undressed, I proceeded to pull my black dress on over my head. I smoothed out any wrinkles and turned to face the rest of the females.

"Oh Layla, you look as good as the goddess herself." Cassia looked me up and down, her eyes wide with awe.

"See, I told you tonight would be fun," Bexi commented as she pulled her shoulder strap up her arm.

"That dress looks like it was made for you." Yariletta smiled at me.

"Thank you." My voice came out as a low whisper. I didn't trust myself to say more without revealing the emotion in my tone. It wasn't often I got compliments from other females, which was no one's fault but my own. I tended to shy away from forming any friendships while I was on a job–and if I was being honest, even when I wasn't on a job.

Anna had attempted to befriend me on many

occasions. She'd sent me gifts she called care packages, she'd called me when I'd been in between jobs just to see how I was doing, and recently Maggie and Claire had started calling me too. They called it a "virtual girls night" when we are all on a holocall together at night in our pajamas. I always found an excuse to leave after a few minutes. It wasn't that I didn't enjoy their company or their strange human traditions, but I just couldn't afford to get too attached. What if it was just a ploy to gain my trust just to betray me later? No, I couldn't have that. I couldn't trust anyone.

I turned and looked in the mirror on the wall. I felt as beautiful as the females claimed I was. I ran my fingers along the fabric and wondered what Bowen might think of me in this dress. Then I quickly pushed that thought away. It was clear he had a thing for me, but I didn't need to have any feelings for him. His opinion of how I looked didn't matter and I liked it that way. This was a job, a very temporary job at that, and in a few short weeks I'd never see that annoyingly handsome male again.

However, I couldn't help but wonder what he'd be wearing tonight. I bet he'd look nice in a tight military uniform. I could pretend to drop something and watch him bend over to pick it up. There wasn't any harm in just looking at a nice butt in a tight uniform was there? I shook my head of those thoughts and joined the other women in sharing compliments of how nice everyone looked.

* * *

Bowen

I stood at the bottom of the grand staircase behind a large vase of flowers on a small side table. The room was filled with a thousand different scents ranging from pleasantly floral to scents that reminded me of bug spray back home.

The flowers in the vase were pleasant enough to keep me sane. I fiddled with my tight collar and smoothed out my military jacket. All the guards wore Dinak dress military uniforms tonight. The uniform was uncomfortable, but I must admit I did look quite sharp.

I smelled the flowers again and wondered when the women would be arriving to the ball. I bet Layla looked ravishing tonight. My tail thumped the ground just thinking about her. I should probably at least try to keep my distance from her. I was broken both inside and out, but there was something about her that drew me in. Besides, she hated me, so it wasn't like she'd ever accept me as her mate. So what was the harm in complimenting her and asking for a dance?

I heard the distinct sound of female laughter and I looked up to see a group of women coming down the stairs. They descended the stairs as a sea of dresses ranging from poofy pink to slender purple; one servant even wore a nicely tailored black suit and had their hair slicked back. I didn't know any of Kach's servants identified as non-binary. Perhaps this was their way of coming out. Either way they looked sleek and I hoped they had fun tonight.

I scanned the servant's faces, looking for the familiar scowl of the woman who held my heart. There she was. Trailing behind the rest of the women, Layla descended the stairs looking more divine than I could have ever imagined.

All time stopped as I took in the sight of her in a tight black dress with a swoop neck, tiny spaghetti straps and a slit that went all the way up her thigh. My fingers itched to touch her exposed blue skin. I wanted to see for myself if she felt as soft as she looked.

Layla wore a black lace bandana on the top of her head that covered her horns and some of her hair. I wondered if I could talk her into taking it off. I'd love to see her hair hanging loose and free around her shoulders.

Somehow, despite time standing still, I blinked and Layla was suddenly standing before me. My mouth was moving. I had said something and Layla had blushed. What did I say? All of my body parts were clearly working but none of them seemed to be connected.

"You don't look too bad yourself, barbarian." She lightly touched my shoulder as she descended the final stair and walked past me. I got a whiff of her scent and thought I might fall to my knees. She was the perfect mix of musky and sweet; she was my own perfect bowl of porridge and I was as helpless as Goldilocks to resist her.

I watched her with my mouth hanging open as she walked away. Her tight ass under her naughty tail swished in perfect time to the melody of my heart. *Wait, she was walking away! I needed to catch up to her!*

"Uh, wait up, sweetheart," I ran after her like a young school boy salivating over his first crush. "Let me buy you a drink. A woman as beautiful as you should have an expensive drink in her hand."

Layla eyed me up and down and I puffed out my chest, trying to look as strong and masculine as possible.

"Look at Bowen's tail going a mile a minute. Layla, you better take him up on his offer before he sprains that thing," Bexi commented and everyone in their group giggled. I didn't mind. I'd make myself a fool for Layla seven days a week if she'd have me.

After Layla finished her inspection of me she gave me her answer. "Well, Barbarian, if you insist. I'll have an ancient blitz."

Ancient Blitz was the Sirret version of a scotch with an orange twist, and that felt like the perfect drink for the perfect woman.

"I'll get that for you right away. Don't go too far now. I'll be back right quick." Goddamn my accent was coming out thick. Layla's gotten me twisted up so tight, I'd nearly forgotten how to speak.

"I never know what that male is saying," I heard Yariletta comment as I walked away.

"You don't need to know what he's saying to know he wants Layla more than his next meal," Bexi added.

"I think he wants Layla to *be* his next meal, if you know what I mean." Even Rali felt the need to comment on my eagerness. I glanced back at the ladies and saw Layla's cheeks had turned a dark blue. Rali was right of course. I'd give anything for the pleasure of tasting the sweetness between Layla's legs. My cock may not be working, but my tongue sure did.

"Rali!" Bexi was flabbergasted at the elder woman's words.

"What? I was young once. Males used to look at me that way too, ya know."

"Gross, it's like listening to my mother talk about her sexual exploits," Yariletta whispered to Bexi. My feline ears caught the whole conversation.

A moment later I returned with Layla's drink and a little more composure.

"My lady," I handed Layla her ancient blitz while I took a sip of the Sirret version of champagne. I was a simple man with simple tastes, and seeing Layla in that dress was certainly something to celebrate.

Classical music started to play and I felt like a third-class man attending a first-class party.

"This music is a bit stuffy if you ask me," I leaned over and whispered to Layla.

"How can music be stuffed?" I held back a laugh. I could spend a lifetime watching her be confused by my idioms.

"It means it's overly formal, no fun."

She nodded her head in agreement.

I tracked Kach's movements as he walked up to Rali and asked her for a dance.

"Of course, Monstair Kach." She placed her hand in his and they waltzed together like two old pros.

"Rali, you've worked here long enough to know that at the servant's ball I'm just Kach."

"Of course," she bowed. I noticed she didn't take him up on his offer of just calling him Kach, and I doubt she ever would. To a seasoned servant, calling Kach anything other than Monstair felt dangerous, even if he invited you to do it.

The song changed from an upbeat classical waltz to a slower melody.

"Come on, everyone! Join in!" Kach waved everyone to the dance floor.

"May I have this dance?" Venpan bowed to Cassia and held out his hand. Cassia smiled up at him, but just as she was about to place her hand in his, Ryla jumped in and grabbed it.

"Me too," she whined.

"Of course," Venpan laughed, and the three of them took to the dance floor together.

Emed walked up to Bexi and grinned. "Would you honor me with a dance, Bexi?"

"I guess you've been a good boy all week," she smirked as she took his hand.

Young Airna was giggling as Drav whispered something in her ear as they whirled around the dance floor, and even the very young Marza was dancing with another young man, both of them clad in fine suits. I guess Marza found the courage to ask his date to the ball after all. This society had its many flaws, but at least it didn't have any weird ideas about homosexuality. The Sirret people really didn't care who you slept with as long as you looked flawless doing it. The only sin you could commit on Ozinda was to be scarred or otherwise deformed.

Now it was my turn to be brave.

"May I have the great honor of sharing this dance with you?" I bowed low and offered Layla my hand. She eyed it but made no move to accept.

"Why should I dance with a barbarian?"

It seemed she would not be so easy to woo tonight. That was fine by me. I liked a challenge. "I would say you owe me, but that wouldn't be very gentlemanly of me."

"Good, there's nothing worse than an impolite barbarian." But she didn't move away from me. In fact, she grinned.

I needed to say something clever, something she wouldn't expect. "Dance with me because I'm a selfish man who wants to be seen with the most beautiful woman in the room." Before she could answer, I took her drink from her hand and set it down on a side table. When I returned, I bowed again and held out my hand. "Please." I wasn't above begging. Layla grinned and placed her hand in mine.

Luckily for me, slow dancing on Ozinda was much the same as slow dancing on Earth. No need to memorize any fancy dance steps, just two people swaying together to the melody of the music.

We walked onto the dance floor and I placed one hand on her shoulder and the other on her hip. She placed both hands on my shoulders and moved as stiffly as my middle school date. I pulled her in a bit closer to me and whispered, "I promise I don't bite, sweetheart."

"I'm not so sure I believe you." Despite her words she loosened up a bit and we swayed together to the music.

"You know, if anything I should be afraid *you'll* bite *me*, after stabbing me and all that." She narrowed her eyes at me just as I expected she would. I loved to see her gray eyes swirl with fire.

"You deserved it." She held her chin up, haughty and proud.

"How so? By doing my job?" I pretended to be insulted.

"By cornering me."

"Ah, I see. I promise to never corner you again."

"I guess even a barbarian like you is capable of learning from his mistakes." She smiled a genuine smile. She loved to win an argument and I loved arguing with her.

We whirled in companionable silence for a while. I did my best to make sure we danced around the entire perimeter of the dance floor. I wanted everyone to see I was dancing with Layla, and with any luck the other men would get the hint that she was off-limits. She was *mine*.

While we made our way around the room Layla glanced at the other couples, but I couldn't keep my eyes off her. Her dress hugged her curves in ways I wish my body could, her scent was intoxicating, and her smile was worth dying a thousand deaths for the privilege of seeing it just once.

Many of the other couples danced with their tails linked. This was a new custom for me, as I had only recently acquired a tail. Seeing as how everyone was doing it, I was sure I wouldn't be committing any cultural faux pax by intertwining my tail with hers. I dared to do so, and loved the feel of her thinner smooth tail against my thicker fuzzier one. Our tails fit together perfectly, just as I suspected our bodies would too.

Layla suddenly froze in the middle of the dance floor. Her eyes went wide, and I knew I'd made the wrong move. It was clear by her reaction that intertwining tails meant a great deal more than just holding hands while dancing. She dropped her hands from my shoulders and backed away.

"I'm feeling thirsty," was the only response she gave me before walking out of the ball entirely.

CHAPTER 11

Latisha

Who did he think he was trying to link tails with me like that? I splashed cold water from the hygiene room sink onto my face. Sure, some people were casual about it and would link tails with just about anyone, but it was a big deal to me, mostly because no one had ever wanted to link tails with me before. It was like a first kiss but somehow more intimate.

The sensation of his soft fluffy tail curling around mine made me feel all warm and fuzzy. That wasn't an emotion I experienced often and it scared me. Physically, It felt like I was being tickled with small gentle touches, and it was much more arousing than I had expected it to be. My sex still throbbed from that one small touch.

I took a deep calming breath. *You're fine. You've been through worse, much worse. He's just a male who thinks he likes you. He doesn't even know you. He thinks you're a servant!* I shook my head and tried to not think about him anymore.

I rejoined the ball and stood along the wall with

Rali and a few other older servants and and watched as everyone else danced the night way. Everyone except Bowen. he stood on the opposite wall eyeing me and slowly drinking his sweet bubbly wine. A while later a few servants approached me ready to leave the ball.

"Hey Layla! A few of us are headed to the rec room to join the after party. You want to come with us?"

"Sure! Sounds fun!" I did my best to sound enthusiastic. In a way I was. I would welcome any distraction that could pull me away from my thoughts about Bowen and his handsome face, soft fur, green eyes...*UGH!*

The loud music of the after-party could be heard from the top of the stairs leading to the basement. The walls vibrated as we descended the steps. Upon entering the rec room I spotted the source of the music, a buzzpad connected to a string of speakers. The music was a series of loud beats with no words or melody.

On a chair next to the speakers Bexi was sitting on Emed's lap making out with him as if they were the only people in the room. On their right there was a group of people dancing wildly to the music. We Sirret's weren't known for our dancing abilities, so they were mostly jumping in the air and pumping their fists.

"Hey come on over! Get some wine!" Vinee waved Yariletta and I walked over to a table full of empty mugs. He poured us each a generous serving of wine.

"That bottle has the Dirgach house symbol on it," I pointed out to Yariletta.

"It's a tradition. The males sneak into house Dirgach every year and steal as many bottles of wines as they can carry for the Servant's Ball after party."

"Dangerous tradition," I commented as I was handed a mug of wine from Vinee.

"The house Dirgach servants do the same to us every year for their summer picnic. We have a truce. They don't tell on us, and we don't tell on them. It keeps things interesting. Besides, it's the merchants who are rivals, not the servants." Yariletta took a sip of her wine and eyed Vinee like she wanted to pounce on him.

I turned to face the room and took a sip of my own wine. Bexi and Emed were still going at it. The group of people dancing next to the speakers seemed to have gotten bigger, and even Cassia and Venpan had joined the party. Cassia was sitting on Venpan's lap. He whispered something in her ear and she held her hand over her mouth as she laughed.

I took another sip of wine and spotted Bowen in the crowd. He had unbuttoned his military jacket, revealing a hard-muscled chest. My fingers itched to touch that chest. I bet he was a nice mix of soft and hard with all that Katsuro fur. Bowen caught me staring and smiled. I quickly looked away and took another sip of wine.

As I gazed around the room I heard an awful

high-pitched sound. Everyone stopped talking and Bowen lowered two fingers from his mouth. Had that sound come from him? He then jumped on the table and announced,

"You want to see some real dancing?"

The music started back up and he did some fancy footwork on the table. I'd never seen anyone's feet move so fast. It was like they were defying gravity. His boots made a satisfying thump every time they made contact with the table. Everyone gathered around and started cheering him on. I found myself at the front of the crowd and clapping along with everyone else.

Bowen and I made eye contact again. Then he moved to my end of the table and kept his eyes locked on me as he continued his strange dance. The rest of the world seemed to fade away and it felt like he was performing just for me. He did a few more hops and stomps before he jumped off the table and landed in a squat with his arms out wide. The world rushed back into focus and I suddenly heard loud cheers from the crowd.

He stood up and walked straight toward me. His chest was out, his tail was swishing, and he had the most arrogant grin on his face. Goddess, he was handsome when he carried himself like that. He pinned me with a possessive stare and my heart raced in my chest with each step he took, closing the gap between us.

"What do ya think? Pretty impressive, huh?" His brow glistened with sweat and his chest was heaving from the exertion of dancing so fast.

"I guess even a barbarian can dance on a good night." I looked at my nails as if they were the most interesting thing in the world, trying to look as unphased as possible.

"Oh yeah? Is that a compliment, Layla?"

"No, it's merely a comment."

"Is that so? Then why don't you dance with this barbarian right now?" He took another step closer and his spicy scent tickled my nose. He was only an inch or two taller than me, but somehow his presence towered over me in a deliciously possessive way. I imagined our bodies pressed together as we danced in the crowd and it made me feel tingly all over. I wanted that. I shouldn't but I did. I was just about to agree to the dance when someone pulled on my arm.

"Come on! We're doing a group dance!" Bexi pulled me into a group of females who were all dancing together next to the speakers. I let her pull me along. This was good. Getting pulled away from Bowen was a good thing, right? If that were true then why did I feel like mourning the dance we didn't get to have?

* * *

Bowen

She was about to say yes, I just knew it. If Bexi hadn't pulled her away we might have been dancing right now–and none of that stuffy ballroom dancing, neither. *Real* dancing. Two people pressed against each other, letting the music and their hips lead the way. I couldn't be too mad though. Sitting at the makeshift bar nursing a mug of wine, watching Layla move in that little black dress was a treat in and of itself.

She was smiling while she danced, but she didn't look happy. Her smile didn't meet her eyes. Who was the real Layla and why did she pretend to be happy when she wasn't? I still had so many unanswered questions about her. She thought I was going to give up, but there was no way in hell I'd do that. I don't think I could quit her if I tried.

Once all the wine was drunk and everyone had partied until the early hours of the morning people started to make their way back to the dorms. Layla was in the crowd headed for the door meaning it was my time to shine. I closed the gap between us and tapped her shoulder.

"May I walk you to your door, sweetheart?" The women's dorm was on the floor above the men's. I had exactly four flights of stairs to woo Layla one last time before the night was over.

She looked me up and down, assessing the situation in that sexy secret spy way she always did.

"I suppose that would be fine."

I looped my arm in a circle and encouraged her to loop her arm through mine. She understood my meaning and sidled up to me. We started our ascent up the stairs and my heart was soring. Just a few days ago Layla had declared that she'd never touch me again, and now here we were walking together arm in arm. Every inch I gained with her was hard-fought, but it was worth it.

I kept our ascent up the stairs as slow as possible. I wanted to draw this out. This smart, beautiful woman was giving me the time of day and I was going to cherish it.

By the time we made it to her door, the hallway was empty. We stood on the landing, and Layla withdrew her arm from mine.

"I enjoyed dancing with you tonight." I leaned against the wall and gave her my best sexy smile.

Layla looked down and fidgeted with her nails. "I don't know that I'd call the experience pleasurable, but I wouldn't say it was bad, either."

"Why don't you come out and say you had a good time tonight? I know you did." *She did, didn't she? God, I hope so.*

She stopped fidgeting with her nails and looked up at me with a real smile that took my breath away. She was radiant as the sun.

She quickly covered her smile with her hand and her cheeks flushed dark blue. I'd never seen her bashful and I didn't know what to do with myself. I wanted to hold her, kiss her, and pour my heart out to her all at once.

Without even thinking I moved closer to her and gently pushed her hand down from her face.

"Have I ever told you how beautiful you are when you smile?" I bent my head and dragged my nose along the column of her neck. "Or how good you smell every moment of every day?"

"No, I don't think you have." Her voice came out breathy, and she raised her hand to her neck to touch where I'd just smelled her. I could scent her arousal. It was sweet and tangy and spicy just like her. If my cock were working I was sure I would be hard as a rock right now.

"Can I kiss you goodnight? Please don't say no because you have to act all tough. I don't think I could take it."

I was mesmerized by her throat as she swallowed hard. I wanted to nip and lick that perfect neck of hers.

"You can kiss me," she whispered as she tilted her head up toward me. My heart was nearly beating out of my chest and I had to remind myself that I wasn't a schoolboy experiencing his first kiss, even though it felt like I was.

The sight of her with her head tilted, eyes closed, and lips parted was breathtaking I wanted to memorize it, paint it, bottle it up somehow. I leaned down and met my lips with hers. As soon as we connected the same bolt of lightening that shot through my veins when we first touched hands shot through my whole body from my ears all the way to my tail. I felt dizzy with emotion for the first time since I was altered, and all of it was joy.

I teased the seam of her lips with my tongue and she welcomed me with a moan. Her tongue danced on mine in what felt like an ancient ritual of lovers who had met in every lifetime over and over again, only to be separated by death.

Every touch of our lips, every meeting of our tongues sent a new wave of electricity and emotion through me. I needed more, I needed every crumb she would give me. Somehow I had a goddess in my arms. I didn't know what power she wielded or what spell she'd cast on me, but I was hers, every fiber of my being was hers, and she could have it all.

Layla pulled away from the kiss, chest heaving with heavy breaths. She had a beautiful dark blue flush to her skin, and I longed to see her flushed like that with my head between her thighs.

She untangled herself from me and opened the door. But before she slipped inside she met my gaze and whispered, "Goodnight, Bowen."

I was left alone in the dimly lit hallway. I leaned my head against the door and let out a deep sigh. I needed to collect myself before I could walk upstairs to bed. I needed to convince myself that this wouldn't be the last time we kissed. I would woo her again.

I felt a tightness in my groin and took a quick glance down my pants. Hmm, still soft. If Layla couldn't get me hard then my cock was truly broken. Ah well, there were other ways to please a woman.

CHAPTER 12

Bowen

Shortly after I had fallen asleep I was greeted by a visitor in my bed. There were soft lips slowly kissing my chest. I could feel someone's tail wrapped tightly around my leg. This mystery person continued to make their way down my chest with soft sensual kisses. I tried to look up to see who the owner of those amazing lips was, but my head felt weighted down. The room was dark and all I could see was a wave of white hair covering someone's face.

The person dragged a blue hand down my chest and let it rest on my abdomen. Their lips got dangerously close to my miraculously hard cock, and my balls felt gloriously tight, a sensation I hadn't felt for a very long time. I hissed as those lips enveloped my cock in a delightful wet heat. The stranger took me deep into their mouth and their head bobbed back up again. I was completely lost to the pleasure of it all. The stranger lowered their head again and again and I was ready to explode. I attempted to lift my head again. I needed to see who this magician was. How did they get my cock to rise? I thought the damage the scientists did was permanent.

I still couldn't see their face, but there was a familiarity to them. I knew this person. The stranger lowered their head onto my cock one last time and sucked.

"Layla," I called out as I came for the first time since my abduction.

I sat up in bed with a start. My chest was heaving. I placed a hand over my heart as if I could somehow stop it from beating so fast.

It was just a dream. It may have been the best dream of my entire existence, but it was still just a dream. The dim morning light was starting to shine through the window, and I lamented that I'd have to get up soon. I wanted more time with my dream lover.

I shifted in bed and felt a warm wetness on the blanket. I pulled the cover back and to my shock, there before me, was my cock as stiff as a board with cum seeping out of the tip. *Oh thank god, my dick isn't broken after all!*

I looked around the room and saw that everyone was still sleeping. I reached into my pants, excited to feel the pump of my fist for the first time in months, when I was pricked by something sharp. *What the fuck?* I pulled my hand back up and watched as a small streak of blood ran down my finger.

I pulled my pants and underwear down far enough to see my cock in the dim light, and to my horror my it was full of barbs.

* * *

Latisha

"Good morning Bexi. I didn't hear you come in last night." Cassia looked up from her embroidery and smiled at the very tired-looking Bexi.

"And you didn't make it to breakfast, either." Yariletta and Cassia exchanged a knowing look.

"I think she was out with Emed." Airna, who was only sixteen years old, did not pick up on the joke that the women all knew who Bexi was with last night.

"Yes I was." Bexi smoothed out her apron before she sat down next to Cassia.

"Well?" Cassia elbowed her.

"Well, what? I wasn't the only one enjoying the company of a romantic partner last night. I saw you making out with Vinee in a dark corner of the rec room," she pointed to Yariletta, "and you were kissing Drav outside in the garden," she pointed to Airna, "and I caught you doing some heavy petting with Venpan in the wine cellar." She elbowed Cassia back.

"I never said I didn't enjoy some physical companionship last night," Cassia confessed. "I was just pointing out that you were the only one who didn't come back to the dorm, and that isn't like you. I know you've been happy to accept Emed into your bed from time to time, but you've never gone to his before."

"So?" Bexi huffed, acting annoyed, but she couldn't hide the small smile that shone on her face.

"So, what happened? Where were you all

night?" Yariletta inquired.

"A proper Sirret female doesn't give away her secrets." Bexi lifted a defiant chin in the air.

"You are not a proper Sirret female, Bexi," Cassia laughed.

Bexi drew in a gasp and held a hand to her chest. "I am too!" She tried her best to look shocked, but soon her chin was quivering and she couldn't hold back her laugh any longer.

"Alright, alright I'll give you the details."

As I attempted to embroider my napkin, once again failing to get any of the stitches right, Bexi described her night. She and Emed went to the roof for some privacy. Emed had brought a blanket with him and apparently they made out for quite some time in the cool breeze of the night. Bexi described how romantic it was to kiss under the stars. Eventually, one thing led to another, and they mated multiple times on the roof.

Her story reminded me of how I, too, had shared a kiss with someone last night: Bowen. His kiss had felt electric, unlike anything I'd experienced before. My whole body had felt on fire from his touch. I throbbed even now just thinking about it. Distracted by thoughts of Bowen and his soft lips on mine, the firm grip of his arms around my waist, and his tongue gliding over mine, I pricked my finger with the sewing needle.

"Ow!" I muttered under my breath.

"You know Layla, I could help you with your stitches. I was just as bad as you until someone showed me how to do it," Cassia offered.

"No, thank you." I forced a smile. I appreciated her offer, but I didn't need help. I could do it on my own, just like everything else in my life.

"Suit yourself," she shrugged.

Cassia reminded me of Anna. They were both self-assured and kind to a fault. Even last night had Anna messaged me on my buzzpad asking how I was doing. She'd sent me a selfie of her frowning saying she missed me and was excited for my return when this job was over. I didn't understand why she would miss me. She was just being nice. I'm sure she sent messages to everyone on the team.

I continued to listen to everyone's stories from last night and struggled with my embroidery. I would figure this out if it was the last thing I did.

＊ ＊ ＊

Bowen

I beat on Krix's door with three hard knocks. It was still the early morning and the sun had not fully risen. Upon discovering my newly barbed cock I had quickly gotten dressed and headed straight for Krix's apartment. I had a lot of urgent questions, the first of which was whether or not these damn things could be removed. Having a barbed cock felt even more useless than a soft one. I still couldn't have sex with anyone, and now I ran the risk of stabbing myself every time I moved too abruptly. If there was a god, I was confident

I was their jester. My life sure did feel like one sick joke at the moment.

I raised my hand to bang on the door again when Krager, Krix's mate, opened the door holding a phase gun.

"What do you want, mutant? My mate isn't awake yet." Krager wore a scowl on her face and I didn't blame her, but my barbed cock truly felt like a worthy emergency.

"I'm sorry to disturb you at this early hour, but I have a bit of a medical emergency."

"Let him in," I heard a sleepy voice call from behind Krager. Krager eyed me again then moved so I could enter her house.

"Thank you. Thank you both." I entered the house and saw Krix in a robe and slippers. Krager was wearing a sports bra and loose shorts. She set the phase gun, which was the size of a hunting rifle back home, against the wall. She leaned against the wall next to the gun and kept her eyes locked on me. I had no doubt that she'd shoot me if she felt her wife was being threatened.

"What seems to be the problem, Bowen? I don't see any blood dripping out of any holes."

I nervously wrung my hands together. "Ah, my issue is more of a delicate matter." I glanced over at Krager who gave no indication that she was going to leave the room any time soon.

"Well come out with it. What's wrong with you? Where are you hurt?" Krix waved her hand, encouraging me to continue on with my explanation.

"I uh, I will need to pull my pants down to show you my...issue." Krager pinched the bridge of her nose and Krix just sighed.

"Fine. Get on with it." Krix waved her hand impatiently.

I unbuttoned my pants and let them drop to the floor. I then pulled my drawers down to reveal my hard barbed cock.

Krager chuckled. "Leave it to a male to say that a hard barbed cock is an emergency."

Krix sighed and motioned for me to sit on her examination table.

"Well, for someone whose cock didn't have barbs yesterday and does today, I would say it *is* an emergency."

"Look on the bright side, Bowen, at least your cock is working again," Krix chuckled.

"Yeah, for all the good it does me. I can't even touch myself, let alone have relations with anyone," I huffed.

"Oh, calm down. I can remove the barbs and you'll be just fine."

"Really? Oh thank god. I thought I was doomed to a lifetime of painful celibacy." I fell back onto the cold table in relief.

"Congratulations Bowen," Krager commented, then she looked to her mate, "I'm going back to bed my kira-si, let me know if you need anything."

"Alright, will do." Krix blew Krager a kiss then turned her attention back to me.

"Who's the lucky person?" She asked as she

gathered the necessary medical supplies from her drawers.

"What do you mean? I don't think anyone would consider themself lucky to be mated to me right now."

"No, no, I mean who did you mate bond with? The Katsuro males only grow barbs on their cock after their body recognizes their bonded mate, and seeing as your half Katsuro, and how you suddenly have barbs on your cock, I figured the same must be true for you. So who are they?"

My tongue suddenly felt stuck to the roof of my mouth. Mate? I had a bonded mate?

Layla. It had to be her. My mind was running at a million miles a minute. That beautiful siren of a woman was *my* mate. Was that why I was so obsessed with her? No, bonded mate or not, she'd have me wrapped around her finger.

"I see you're still putting two and two together. Well, I hope she's a friend of yours because you're going to be hard for the next five days."

"Five days?" My cock had gone from a soft noodle to an irrepressible stiff board. I couldn't imagine Layla would be interested in correcting that situation. A kiss at the end of the night after we'd attended a ball was one thing, confessing that she was my mate and asking her to have sex with me for the next five days was quite another.

As a matter of fact, I wasn't going to tell Layla she was my mate at all. I didn't think she hated me anymore, but I also didn't think she was ready to admit she liked me either. It was nearly a guarantee that if I told her she was my mate she'd run for the hills. I would just have to play it cool and suffer through the next five days without her assistance.

CHAPTER 13

Latisha

"Hush everyone! He's coming." All the servants were lined up at the bottom of the grand staircase. Kach liked to do a weekly inspection of his staff. The term "inspection" might be too strong. What he was really doing was boosting his ego by walking past the only beings on Ozinda who would call him Monstair.

"Good morning, Monstair Kach." The first Sirret he passed bowed.

"Monstair Kach." The next Sirret bowed.

"Monstair." On and on it went until Kach had walked by everyone.

I had gotten in line next to Bexi, and of course, Bowen had gotten in line next to me. Being so close to him reminded me of our kiss. I still didn't know how I had been able to pull away from him. I had wanted to keep going when I found the strength to untangle myself from his grasp.

"You look like you've got a lot on your mind this morning." Bowen leaned down and whispered so only I could hear. His voice sounded strained today, his face pinched with pain as he straightened himself back up and smoothed any wrinkles out of his uniform.

"What does it matter to you, Barbarian?" My words came out harsher than I had anticipated. A part of me was angry that I would never have the chance to develop a real relationship with Bowen. I forced myself to remember this was all temporary and someday soon Bowen would be a distant memory.

"So you do have a lot on your mind," he looked down at me and smirked. That smirk made me want to stab him again. How was he so impervious to all my harsh edges? I'd made countless other males cower with my glare and harsh tone, but everything I threw at Bowen seemed to roll off him like a droplet of water.

"Thank you everyone for gathering here today. Your presence is appreciated as always," Kach began.

"Our presence is required," Bowen grumbled.

"As you well know, the servant's ball was quite the success, and from everyone's smiling faces I can tell you all thoroughly enjoyed yourselves. I am sad to report, however, that the expenditures from the ball were higher than I had anticipated. That being said, I will have to cut everyone's pay this week by just a fraction."

"He does this every year," Yariletta sighed.

"I know you are a resilient bunch and will crack on just fine." Kach looked around the room at his dutiful servants who could do nothing about their reduction in pay. "That's all. You can get on with your work." He waved us on and all the servants filed out, grumbling along the way.

Bowen didn't have his graceful gait today. He hobbled as he walked out of the room and his normally controlled tail thrashed behind him. I wondered what was ailing him this morning. Maybe he'd been wounded on guard duty. It wasn't really any of my concern.

I had to admit, even with his gamely hobble his butt still looked good enough to squeeze. I bet it would look even better with a red handprint on it. I bet his pale human skin left a delicious red mark after being handled roughly. The thought of his bare ass had me hot and bothered all over again.

"You coming?" Bexi yelled for me disrupting my thoughts.

"Yeah, I'll be right there." I rushed to the hygiene room and splashed cold water on my face. I needed to get these images of Bowen out of my head. A thought suddenly occurred to me. I pulled my buzzpad out of my pocket, checked the calendar, and sighed with relief. My rut was coming up soon. No wonder I was so affected by Bowen. It was just hormones, nothing more. Once my rut passed Bowen would be as intriguing to me as a bland bowl of soup. I put my phone back in my pocket and left the hygiene room feeling light and unburdened.

A day later I was sitting with the female servants failing to embroider my napkins once again when Yariletta sat down and joined us.

"Good afternoon. It's nice to have you back with us," Bexi commented.

"Yeah, my rut came early this month," Yariletta

sighed.

"Oh, who'd you spend it with? Vinee?," Cassia inquired as she deftly completed another flower on her cloth napkin.

"You two were making out at the after party just a few days ago," Bexi added.

"No," Yarlietta let out a disappointed sigh. "I spent my rut alone. What Vinee and I have is too new, and he knew my rut was coming soon before we started flirting. I told him he'd have to wait until next month to be my rutting partner. I just want to make sure he wasn't flirting with me just to rut and never speak again."

"Alone! I could never! I'd be humping every object in the room."

"Bexi!" Cassia held a shocked hand to her chest. "That's a little crude, don't you think?"

"Who do you spend your ruts with?" Yariletta ignored Cassia's shocked reaction.

"I have a male friend whose six month rut usually falls in line with my monthly one. He helps me through my rut and I help him through his. Well, that is until Emed and I started getting serious. I suppose now that we're a thing, I'll spend my rut with him." Bexi smiled down at her sewing.

"That's a clever idea. I hadn't thought of that before." Yariletta furrowed her brows in contemplation.

At least I won't have to pretend I'm rutting this month. As an allgender female who only rutted once every six months, I had to spend my late adolescence pretending I had my rut. I would pick a random day at the end of the month, shut myself away for the day, and hoped no one would question me about it. Unfortunately, I was always questioned about it. Rutting was new and exciting for the young Sirrets I hung out with and all the females had a habit of asking each other how their rut went. I learned how to get good at lying during that time.

Bexi did bring up an interesting point about having a rutting partner. I wondered if Bowen would...*no*, I couldn't think about that. Even though I'd caught him sniffing me twice yesterday, I didn't think he'd be interested in mating me if he knew I was an allgender. I didn't even know if they had allgenders where he was from.

"Vinee did tell me some interesting news about the rebellion." Yariletta's comment brought me out of my thoughts.

"What did he say?" Bexi whisper-shouted.

Yariletta leaned in and whispered, "The Junak is asking everyone to gather in the city square at midnight on Flower Day."

"Flower Day, huh? That's clever," Cassia commented.

"The Junak is a smart male," Yariletta smiled.

"One of the few," Bexi laughed.

Mounting an attack on Flower Day would send a strong message. It would mark the 150th anniversary of the last uprising. The merchant class struck down that rebellion with an iron fist. More than half of the laborers were jailed and placed in labor campus. Then they were given just enough food to keep working. They didn't want their labor force to starve to death, but they didn't want them to have the energy to escape either.

The merchants released the labors ten years later. Stories of their return home have been passed down through the generations. The sight of the once strong rebels coming back beaten and weak demoralized anyone who still wished to fight.

"Hush, someone's coming," Cassia shushed them. Heavy footsteps sounded throughout the hall. As they drew closer I caught sight of Bowen's orange and brown-furred arms coming down the hallway. Bowen walked into the room with his usual arrogant smile. He was back to his normal self, standing tall, and walking with graceful strides.

"Good afternoon," he gave a deep bow that just so happened to land his nose inches from my shoulder. He let out what sounded like a pained gasp. He stood up straight and his eyes were as wide as saucers.

"Are you alright, Bowen?" Cassia asked.

He looked at me with that shocked expression on his face. "I, uh, I have to go." He turned and abruptly left the room.

"That male is so strange," Bexi commented before returning to her sewing. Bowen was strange, but it was not like him to suddenly lose all of his confidence and run out of a room. I wondered if something was really bothering him.

I should investigate. Maybe his strange

behavior was connected to the rebellion somehow. My justification seemed weak even to me but I was too curious to let this go.

CHAPTER 14

Latisha

I assumed from the direction he'd went, he ran to the male's dorm. I took to the stairs and found myself quietly stepping up to the dorm door. I put my ear up to the wood and heard someone moaning inside. Was he ill?

I opened the door just enough to see what kind of state Bowen was in. He was sitting up in bed with his back to me. His arm was moving in quick up-and-down motions and he moaned again.

"Layla," he breathed.

Was he...was he pleasuring himself to thoughts of me? I was strangely flattered by this new development. I should back away, close the door, and never think about this again, but something was holding me in place. He moaned my name again, and I felt tingly all over. My horns itched and a familiar throbbing started between my thighs. I wanted to hear him say my name my real name, not my alias.

Suddenly my chest was vibrating and a loud purring filled the room. Bif me! I was purring! My rut came early!

Bowen's arm froze and he whipped around to see me standing in the doorway. I slammed the door and ran down the stairs. I was only a quarter of the way down before Bowen came running after me.

"Layla, wait!"

I did not. I shouldn't have stayed in that room. I should have backed away and left when I had the chance; now he knew that I knew he was pleasuring himself to thoughts of me. Once he caught up to me he'd hear me purring and I didn't want to find out what would happen after that. Would he tease me? Make fun of me? Brag that he had a powerful effect on females?

I made it to the landing on the second floor when Bowen jumped down in front of me.

"Would you wait a damn minute?" He leaned onto the railing as he caught his breath. "Let me explain." He reached out and squeezed my shoulder. His touch was meant to be a friendly gesture, but instead, it made the dull ache between my legs turn into a deep throb.

He opened his mouth to say more, but he closed it again. I was purring. Loudly. "Are you rutting?"

"Yes," I sighed. "My rut has come early." This was awful. I was aching, I wanted to go suffer alone somewhere, but most of all I wanted Bowen to touch me. *Ugh! These damn hormones!*

"I'm ah, going through a kind of rut myself." He raked a hand through his hair and bit the corner of his mouth while he pondered the situation.

He snapped his fingers, "I've got an idea! Why

don't we help each other out? You're going through a rut, I'm going through a rut, there's no reason why we have to suffer alone when we could ease our needs together."

I opened my mouth to reject him, but then the conversation with Yariletta played through my head. She had a friend who was a rutting partner. They way she told it, they weren't romantically involved, they just used each other to ease their suffering. This could work. As long as Bowen didn't reject me because I was an allgender, this might actually be pleasurable.

"Fine, but we're just friends helping each other out, nothing more." I held up a defiant chin waiting for him to argue with me.

"Sounds fine to me. Friends with benefits, that's it."

Friends with benefits. I liked that.

"Let's go to the spare room then." The spare room on the top floor of the mortress was reserved for Sirret servants going through their rut.

Bowen's tail whacked the floor so hard that I jumped. He quickly grabbed it, and extended his hand. "After you."

We got to the room at the top of the stairs. It was small but clean. The sheets were fresh and the bed was neatly made. The hygiene room was well stocked, and the thick curtains that hung over the window were closed. Everything was in order. The only thing that felt out of place in this room was me. The purring in my chest and the ache between my thighs told me that my body wanted this. I wanted to spend my rut with Bowen. But the voice inside my head that warned me to not trust anyone was making me rethink this decision. I already liked Bowen a great deal more than I should; would rutting with him blur that line even more? Ever since my mother's betrayal, I'd fought to keep myself emotionally distant from everyone, and yet here was this handsome cat man who had taken down nearly every wall I'd so painstakingly built over the years.

Bowen leaned against the opposite wall trying to look unbothered, but his twitching ears gave him away. "So, how do you want to do this?"

Oh no, this was really happening. We were really talking about how we wanted to proceed with our mating. My heart raced and my palms grew sweaty. I'd have to take my clothes off, and he'd see that I was an allgender. I still hadn't figured out if his people had something like that.

My face must have given away my panic because Bowen stood up from the wall and took a step toward me. "Boundaries! We should set boundaries," he suddenly blurted out.

His declaration disrupted my panicked thoughts. Boundaries? That might make things more comfortable for me. But what boundaries did I have? Should I make something up?

At my hesitation, Bowen shared his own boundaries. "You might have guessed, but I personally don't have a lot of boundaries." He gave me that cocky grin of his.

"I don't do degradation though," he frowned.

"It just doesn't sit right with me saying mean things to someone you're having relations with. And I may be a man, but even I enjoy being called a good boy from time to time." His tail wacked the floor again. I think he liked being called a good boy much more than he led on. "What about you? What are your boundaries?"

No one had ever asked me what my boundaries were before. My other lovers would just kiss me for a while then have me turn around while they bent me over the bed or took me against a wall.

Boundaries, boundaries... "Touching! I don't want there to be a lot of touching!" There, that was easy enough. Memories of Bowen caressing my tail during our card game flashed before me, and my purring grew even louder. There was no way I could be caressed by Bowen like that and leave here not wanting more of him. If he didn't touch me very much this might feel more clinical, more like what I'd experienced in the past, and although those experiences weren't that great, at least I'd be able to remain emotionally distant from Bowen.

"Umm ok, anything in particular you don't like?" He wrung his hands together, and for the first time, he looked nervous.

"I'll let you know if I don't like something."

"Okay, sounds good to me," Bowen gave me a pinched smile and I noticed for the first time a very large bulge in his pants. "Should we get started then?" He started to pull his pants down when panic flooded through me again.

"Wait!" I held up a hand. He stopped. I braced

myself for him to be angry with me, but instead, he just looked concerned. "There's something you should know about me before we get started."

"Okay," he looked at me expectantly while he held his unbuttoned pants up around his waist.

"I'm different from most Sirret females."

"Tell me something I don't know." He laughed, but when he saw that I wasn't smiling, he stopped. "Look, whatever it is, I'm sure it's fine." He gave me a reassuring smile.

"We'll see," I huffed, and my tail twitched behind me. "I...do they have allgenders on your homeworld?"

His brows furrowed. "Allgender...allgender... where have I heard that word before?" He snapped his fingers, "That's right! Allgenders are intersex people right?"

"Intersex?" That was a new term for me.

"Yeah, you know, people born with anatomy outside of the binary. Like they might have both female and male parts."

So his people did have allgenders. That was a little reassuring.

"How do you view allgender–or intersex people, as you call them?"

"How do I view them?" He looked surprised at my question. "Well they're just people, and it's not like they're all the same. On Earth at least, there's a wide range of what it means to be intersex." His brows furrowed as he thought about it some more. "I'm not put off by the idea of intersex people, if that's what you're asking. I'm what my homeworld calls a bisexual, which means I've lain with both men and women and enjoyed it." His wicked grin was back on his face. He was proud to be this...bisexual orientation. I knew there were Sirrets who liked both males and females, but here on Ozinda that wasn't a recognized sexual preference. The Sirret people had a belief that if you claimed to like both genders you just hadn't made up your mind yet. To be bisexual, as Bowen called it, was the same as saying you were indecisive about who you preferred, and no one would ever take you seriously. I liked the idea that he was bisexual. Maybe he wouldn't mind my uniqueness after all.

He snapped his fingers again as realization dawned on him. "You're an allgender aren't you? Is that why you're asking me about this?"

I wasn't brave enough to speak so I just nodded my head.

His brows furrowed in a very serious look. "I know how your society treats people who are viewed as different. If you're afraid I'm not going to want to have sex with you because you're an allgender you're dead wrong. You've got me so twisted in knots I'm going to spend the rest of my life untangling myself from you."

His words sent a shiver down my spine. He cut the distance between us with one step. Then he lifted my hair to his nose and sniffed as if it were a drug he was addicted to. "I'm going to want you no matter what's between your legs. Now, are you going to take off that dress or are you fixin' to drive me wild by making me wait?"

He was all confidence, and he looked down at me as if he already knew I had the courage to reveal myself to him even if I didn't know it yet. My purring grew louder at his closeness and my body felt achy and sensitive.

I untied my apron before I could lose my nerve. Bowen's eyes were locked on me as I let my apron fall to the floor. I turned around and asked, "Will you unzip me?"

He gently pushed my long hair over my shoulder. His finger slid up my collarbone then he slowly dragged that one sensuous finger down my spin until it met the zipper. He leaned down and brushed his lips against my bare neck before he pulled down my zipper. Every touch made my skin hum. I wanted more, so much more that it scared me.

With my servant's dress unzipped Bowen slid his finger under the sleeve and then proceeded to pull it down my arm. Despite the large insistent bulge in his pants, he was taking his time. He seemed to enjoy touching me as much as I enjoyed being touched.

I pushed my other sleeve down and let the dress fall to the floor. My breasts were small for a Sirret female so I didn't wear any chest support garments. Still facing away from him, I pulled my underwear down my legs and let the cloth fall to the floor as well.

It was the moment of truth. I'd find out if Bowen really liked me as an allgender or not. I turned around to face him and his heated gaze traveled up and down my naked body. I was tempted to cover my sex, but what would be the point? I needed to get this over with. Either Bowen liked my body or he didn't. I'd experienced rejection before; I could suffer through it again.

He drew in a raspy breath as if he'd forgotten how to breathe.

"Sweetheart, you might just be the most beautiful woman I've ever seen." He swallowed hard as he looked over me again. "Is that your preferred gender? Now that I know you're an allgender, I can call you whatever you prefer."

Not only did he like my body, but he'd be willing to accept if I saw myself outside of the binary? This male was truly an alien here on Ozinda.

"I identify as a female." I let my voice dip to its natural tenor. I liked my voice, its deep cadence felt commanding as it rumbled through my own chest.

Bowen leaned against the wall as if he suddenly needed the support. "Damn woman, is that your real voice? You're a real Miley Cyrus, Cher combo aren't you?" I didn't know who those people were, but from the way Bowen was affected by my voice it was safe to assume he liked it. This was going surprisingly well.

"My perilla doesn't bother you?" I had to confirm that this was all real, that he was really telling the truth.

"Your perilla? Oh right, Sirret women don't have a clit. Sweetheart, you look perfect to me. Human women have a sensitive bud of flesh in the same place you do, we call it a clit. Yours is a little bigger, but beautiful all the same."

I...wow. This was real. He really did like my body.

"It's your turn." I pointed to him.

"Right." He looked down at his hand still clutching his unbuttoned pants. He let them fall to the floor. Then he pulled his shirt off over his head. Lastly, he pulled his underwear down to reveal a large erect cock studded with small bumps from the tip to the base. My channel clenched on nothing at the sight of it. It wasn't hard to imagine that he would feel amazing inside me.

"So what did you have in mind, Layla?" His voice came out as a strained rasp. "How can I help you through your rut?"

I wanted to suggest we mate on the bed. I've always wanted to mate face-to-face, but I didn't want to push my luck. I leaned over the bed with my butt high in the air. "How about this?" I would stick to what I was familiar with. For better or for worse, it felt like the safest option.

"If that's what you prefer." Bowen raked a hand through his short brown hair and strode up to the bed. "Why don't you go ahead and lay down on the bed so I can work my foreplay magic." He did his strange eye twitch and smiled, his old confidence coming back to him again.

"What is foreplay?" I was unfamiliar with this human term.

"Uh, it's where I get the pleasure of licking that sweet pussy of yours until you're wet enough to receive me." He licked his lips in anticipation of such an action.

An image flashed before me of Bowen's face pinched with disgust as he saw my perilla up close. He claimed to like my body, but I wasn't brave enough to cross that line yet. It felt too risky.

"I'm ready, no foreplay needed." It was true. Thanks to the hormones provided by my rut, I was already wet enough to take him.

Bowen's lips turned down in an adorable frown. "But that's half the fun."

I glanced down at his hard studded cock and my sex clenched again. I was painfully throbbing with need and I wanted him now.

"I need you now, Barbarian." It took all the courage I could muster to confess I needed him, but that was better than him seeing my perilla during this foreplay he described.

He shrugged his shoulders. "Your wish is my command." Command...I'd like to command him.

He stepped even closer to me. I could feel his thighs touching mine and I shuddered with anticipation of what was to come.

He slowly caressed my back with the most gentle touch anyone had ever given me. Tracing my spine with his finger, he went all the way down to the base of my tail. He slid his hand up and down the sensitive base and I moaned with pleasure. Was it possible to come from someone stroking my tail, because I just might.

"Does this feel good?" He whispered into my ear

as if we were sharing a secret. All I could do was nod my head. He slid his hand up and down the base of my tail again, and my hips twitched, seeking out more of his touch.

"Bowen." His name came out as a whine.

"I've got you, sweetheart. I'm going to take good care of you." He stroked my tail a few more times before wrapping it around his waist. "I need to move your tail a little, is this comfortable?" No one had ever inquired about my comfort during sex before and I wasn't prepared to give an answer.

"Wher-wherever is fine," I stuttered.

"Wherever is certainly not fine," he growled. He slid my tail a little further up his chest, and I knew he'd probably have to lean in an awkward way because of it.

"Is that going to be comfortable for you?" I couldn't help but ask.

"My comfort is of little concern here. As long as my cock can reach your pussy, I'll be a happy man."

I started to protest but the words died in my throat as he slid his cock along my sex, coating himself with my natural lubricant. A startled gasp escaped my lips.

"Are you alright there, sweetheart?" His words came out strained.

"Ye-yes," I gasped as he slid his cock through my sex again. I'd never felt so needy in my entire life. Never had a rut been so intense before. I felt overly sensitive and my whole body felt like it was on fire.

"Please," I whimpered. I expected him to have

some witty response to my plea, but all he could manage was a low growl.

He notched his cock at my entrance and slowly sank into me. I felt every raised bump on his shaft as it passed through my channel, and every bump sent me closer and closer to the edge. Once he was fully seated in me he let out a shuddering breath.

"You are a goddess, Layla, and no one can tell me different."

I heard the strain in his voice and prepared myself for him to go crazy with quick rough thrusts now that he was inside of me, but he didn't. Again he took his time slowly pulling out of me and slowly pushing back again. I wasn't a virgin but I certainly felt like one in this moment. I'd never experienced pleasure like this during a mating. Bowen filled me again and I felt every raised bump wash over every nerve ending in my channel.

He stroked my back as he shifted in and out of me. Of all the sensations I was feeling, that one hand drifting up and down my back felt the most intimate. I had experienced intercourse before, although nothing like this, and I had experienced touch through a male's rough grip on my hips, but I had never experienced touch like this. No one had taken the time to caress me while they took their own pleasure pumping into my slick channel.

"Perfect, you're so perfect," he breathed. It all felt like too much. It was too intimate and too vulnerable. I was feeling things about Bowen that I'd never felt for anyone before. *Don't trust anyone.* The words rang through my head like an alarm warning me of danger.

"Stop, stop, stop," I commanded as I froze, not sure how he would respond.

Bowen immediately stopped and pulled out of me. I stood and backed away from him. He'd always seemed very calm and collected, but I saw how painfully hard he was earlier, and this might prove to be too much for him. He was of course still erect, and seeing his studded cock made my sex throb all over again. My body and my mind definitely were not in the same place at the moment. Mentally I wanted to run away from the vulnerability I was feeling, but physically I wanted to feel him push into me again and again.

"Layla? Is everything ok?" Bowen asked with concern written all over his face.

Right, he didn't even know my real name. The only real thing he knew about me was that I was an allgender. He didn't know my history, who I really worked for, or why I was really here. I could work with that. This didn't have to be emotional. I was rutting and he was rutting. This was just a need, just a scratch to be itched, and Bowen just so happened to be the best person for the job.

"Thank you for stopping." I was grateful that he'd stopped. He could have just as easily forced me to keep going.

"Don't thank me for that," he growled. "Never thank me for stopping when you've asked me to. No means no. It doesn't matter where you're at in doing the deed. I'm not concerned about my cock right now, I'm concerned about you. Are you alright? Did I hurt you?"

His concern for me made my heart squeeze, and I had to remind myself again that this wasn't emotional, it was just a physical need.

"I'm fine. It's just you do too much talking. I don't like all your compliments and touches and caresses." Maybe I could get through this without getting too attached to Bowen if he treated me a little more like all the other males had.

"So you're saying I'm too nice, is that it?"

"Yes, stop that."

Bowen looked down and pinched the bridge of his nose. "And no touching," I added.

"Layla." My alias came out in a tone of exacerbation.

"What? It's not that hard. I'll bend over next to the wall and you can brace your hand on it." I crossed my arms over my chest and gave Bowen a determined scowl.

"Layla, have you had sex before?" Bowen's hands were on his hips as if he were about to scold me like a youngling.

"Yes, I've had sex before!" Why would he think I hadn't mated before?

"And what you just described, the no touching, and not saying nice things, is that what it was like?"

"I don't see what that has to do with this," I huffed.

"It has everything to do with this." He closed

the gap between us with his dark feral gaze locked on me. "When you had sex before, did the men not touch you?"

I wanted to say something clever, or at the very least something insulting, but the way he looked at me with hungry eyes and a tightly clenched jaw made my heart flutter. My silence was enough of an answer for him.

"Give me their names," he growled.

That was an odd request. "Why?"

"Because they will pay for making you feel anything less than the beautiful, perfect woman that you are."

"It's not that important," I sighed. "Let's just move on."

"It's important to me," he growled.

"Well, it shouldn't be. I'm having my rut and you're having yours. That's all this is, friends with benefits just like you said."

His mouth turned down in a frown. "That might be true but I'm not going to treat you like those other men did. You might be used to that kind of thing, but you better get ready to broaden your horizons because I'm fixing to introduce you to something much better."

Bowen fell to his knees before me and wrapped his big strong hands around the back of my thighs. He pulled me toward him and my gaze fixated on his soft lips. I put my hand on his hand and luxuriated in the feel of his impossibly soft hair between his catlike ears.

He looked up at me with those piercing green eyes and pulled me even closer to him, my sex now mere inches from his face, his lips.

"Tell me to stop, Layla. Tell me you don't want this and I'll back away." His eyes softened and he pleaded, "Please let me pleasure you." I wished he would give me a determined look instead of those soft pleading eyes. I wanted his fierce stubbornness. I wanted to feel like he was challenging me to say no, but he wasn't. He was pleading with me, begging to give me something that I'd wanted my entire adult life.

My breath quickened as he continued to look at me like I was the greatest thing in the universe. This was the closest anyone had gotten to my perilla and not only was he not disgusted, he looked excited. I *did* want this. I wanted someone to enjoy my unique body just as much as I did. No, I didn't want just anybody to enjoy my body, I wanted Bowen, just Bowen.

I'd give in this one time, then I'd put my guard back up. Bowen would get what he wanted, I'd be mean to him later, and he wouldn't bother me again. It'd be fine. This was just an itch and Bowen was just the scratcher.

"I want that," I breathed. Before I could even get the last syllable out, Bowen had descended upon me. He licked my sex and moaned as if my essence were the greatest thing he'd ever consumed. His tongue drew a line from the bottom of my sex all the way up to my perilla. I gasped as soon as I felt his tongue make contact with my sensitive flesh. My knees felt weak and if he hadn't been holding me up I would have surely fallen.

CHAPTER 15

Bowen

God, Layla tasted sweet on my tongue. I didn't think I'd ever get enough of her, enough of *this*. I dragged my tongue up and down her wet pussy again. Her hand on my head gripped my hair deliciously tight. She spurred me on with her moans. I was going to give her the best sexual experience of her life. Unfortunately, that wasn't a high bar in her case.

I dragged my tongue up her sex again and circled it around the large bud of flesh she called a perilla. A garbled cry released from her throat and something feral snapped inside me. I wanted more of her sounds. I wanted her legs shaking from my touch. I wanted my name falling from her lips.

I circled her perilla again and again, wringing moan after moan out of her. I experimentally drew a figure-eight pattern on her sensitive flesh and her hips bucked, shoving her bud into my mouth, and I kept it there. I didn't suck on it, not yet. I wanted to draw out her pleasure, and selfishly I wanted to taste her on my tongue for as long as possible.

I flicked my tongue back and forth over her perilla and she let out another garbled cry. I flicked my tongue again and again until her legs trembled in my hands. She was panting my name now. It sounded like a prayer coming from her lips.

I stopped the movement of my tongue and she whined, "Please. I'm so close."

How could I deny her? I pumped the base of her tail with one hand and held tightly to her thigh with my other. I sucked on her sensitive bud and this time my name wasn't a whispered prayer falling from her lips, it was a shout, a cry of release, a roar of victory.

Her knees buckled and she fell into my lap. She gave me a contented smile and allowed herself to lean into my embrace. I dragged my finger down her cheek. She looked away and got to her feet. She walked a few steps to the bed and collapsed again.

I joined her there and we both laid side-by-side regaining our composure. God, she tasted good. Never has a vagina been so delicious before. I wanted more. I wondered if she'd let me have more. She was surprisingly skittish about being touched for someone so fierce. This society and its damned views on body image. I just knew the men she had been with before hadn't treated her right. If they had I'd be the one bent over the bed right now, ain't no doubt about it. My cock twitched at the thought of being pegged by Layla. What a great day that would be.

The truth was I had no idea if there would be a next time for us after her rut. Layla didn't let anyone in emotionally, including me. It was probably for the best. She deserved better than a broken man like me. In the meantime, however, I was more than happy to be used as her personal sex toy.

Her purring had died down and was replaced by the growling of her empty stomach.

"It seems that in our haste we forgot to grab any food to bring with us." I pointed out to Layla who was still lying down. Her response was a low groan.

"I'm just as sad about it as you are," I laughed. "I'll tell you what, I'll go grab some food if you promise to be a good girl and stay right here." Her tail thumped on the bed and I suspected she liked being called a good girl just as much as I liked being told I was a good boy. Her eyes were shut but she had a small grin on her face. "Well, what do you say?"

"I'll stay." Although she kept her eyes closed her grin was undeniable now. My heart soared every time I saw it. Was this what an Olympian felt when they won the gold?

With her promise to remain where she was, I donned my pants and left the room in search of sustenance. I snuck into the pantry and gathered a small amount of a variety of foods in hopes their departure wouldn't be noticed. On my way back up to the room I passed a small side table with a vase full of flowers. Ah, what the hell, might as well grab those, too. Maybe Layla liked receiving flowers.

I breathed a sigh of relief when I opened the door and saw Layla standing in front of the window. I was slightly disappointed to see she had put her servant's dress back on, but at least she was still here.

I set the food down on the small table in the room and was pleased to see the spread I had provided. There was cheese, bread, fruit, and some meat sandwiches I had quickly put together downstairs.

"This is a regular Sunday spread if you ask me. We're just missing a casserole and some cornbread." I sat down across from Layla who was already sampling the cheese and fruit.

"Do you miss your home world?" she asked between bites. My breath caught in my throat. This was the first personal question Layla had ever asked me. Internally I did a little happy dance as I repeated *she likes me*, over and over again in my head.

"No, I don't miss home. Not really. I was trapped on Earth because I didn't have any money to get out of my poor living situation, and now I'm trapped here because I'm an indebted servant to Kach. It feels like I just went from one holler to another," I laughed. "I got stolen from my bed and taken to a whole new galaxy just to discover it's all the same. No one looks out for you and unless you're born rich, you're always gonna be poor."

"Maybe the rebellion will be successful and that won't be the case anymore," she remarked as she started on her bread.

"That could happen. Humans have had many successful rebellions over the course of our history. Unfortunately, it never seems to last long. Eventually the rich always get the upper hand again."

"That's because your people are barbarians. My people wouldn't let the rich take control again." I wanted to be offended but when I looked up Layla was smiling.

"Are you teasing me, Layla? You better watch out, I might just punish you for that."

Her cheeks flushed a dark blue and I could smell the sweet aroma of her arousal fill the room. I wanted to touch those cheeks of hers. There was a thread hanging loose from her bandana, and I took the opportunity to pull it free and touch her skin with the back of my hand.

"Looks like this is coming loose." I pulled the thread and accidentally pulled her whole bandana off. Layla's eyes grew wide and time felt like it was moving in slow motion as she yelled "No!" and I finally saw why she'd never taken her bandana off before.

＊ ＊ ＊

Latisha

Bowen growled as my bandana hit the floor. *Bif me!* My bandana has stayed secured to my head through dancing, sex, and running through the street, but Bowen pulled one tiny thread and the whole thing came loose.

"Who did this to you," he growled low in his throat, his tail lashing behind him.

He suddenly stood from the table and picked up his belt from where he'd left it on the floor.

"What are you doing?" Were my horns so horrible to look at that he had to leave right now?

"Who are they, where do they live?" He took

out a knife from his belt, inspected it then holstered it again. Oh, he wasn't leaving because he found my horns ugly, he was leaving to seek vengeance. That was... incredibly arousing.

I tried to diffuse the situation with a joke. "Those scientists really made you crazy, didn't they?"

"They didn't make me crazy, they just gave me claws." He unsheathed said claws and inspected them, too. "Who are they?" He focused his gaze on me.

Flashbacks of my mother sitting on the floor while her drug dealer cut off my horns ran through my mind. The emotional pain of that day still lingered after all these years.

"Sit down," I patted the bed.

His gaze darkened. "Who, Layla?" He wasn't giving this up. He was dressed and ready to fight for me once again, and for the first time, I actually wanted to tell someone the truth about me. I might regret it later, but I decided to tell him the truth.

"My mother. Well, her drug dealer, but she just sat there while it happened."

Bowen clenched his jaw and walked toward me. "Are they still alive?"

"No." My mother had died from an overdose about a year after the incident, and Bogden died a few years later over a territory dispute.

"Good." Bowen's shoulders relaxed. "But to be honest I would have liked to kill them myself." He reached for my horns and I expected him to run his fingers over them, but instead, he ran his fingers through my hair.

"I can't tell you how long I've waited to see you without that bandana on."

My breath stuttered. I hadn't expected that. I'd expected him to be horrified by my broken horns or look at me with pity, but instead, he just saw me.

Sitting on the bed, I was slightly above eye level with a large bulge in his pants. I wanted to see him naked again. Even now Bowen was so calm and unrattled. I wanted to see what he looked like when he was utterly undone.

My fingers clasped his belt and I undid the fastener. *Thump.* It landed on the floor. His eyes were full of heat as he watched me move to unbutton his pants. Thankfully his shirt was still off. I undid the last button and let his pants fall to the floor as well.

His cock sprang forth and I admired it and its studded beauty. I licked my lips, eager for my turn to scratch this itch for Bowen. Pulling his hips closer I gave his cock one long lick from the base to the tip.

"Layla," he breathed.

"Don't call me that." I wanted to hear my real name. I needed him to know who it was that was bringing him pleasure.

"What do you want me to call you?"

"Latisha. Layla is just a nickname."

"Well, aren't you just full of surprises," he chuckled.

His chuckle turned into a gasp as I licked his shaft again. His hand went to my head and he tangled his fingers in my hair.

I wanted to tease him for a bit. I wanted to

know how long it would take before he started to beg. I ran my hands up and down his thighs. His strong muscles were covered in a fine fur that was soft to the touch. Up and down my hands went, enjoying every inch of him. I let my fingers glide across his sack before my hands went back down again.

"Latisha," he breathed. I loved the sound of my name on his lips. I wanted to hear it again.

I squeezed his ass hard enough that my nails were sure to leave a mark. I licked him up and down again and again until he was panting.

"Latisha." My name was a plea, a cry for mercy.

I smiled to myself and dragged my thumb over the tip of his cock. His breath stuttered and he bucked his hips, shoving his cock into my hand. I held it there for a moment before I fully circled my hand around his length. I gave him one rough tug that caused him to gasp. Then I stroked him up and down slowly.

"Yes," he moaned, his expression finally turning to one of pleasure.

As each bump on his shaft passed through my fingers I remembered how good he felt inside of me and I started to purr again. My channel yearned to be filled and my perilla ached to be touched, but I could wait. I would see Bowen undone before I would let him touch me again.

CHAPTER 16

Bowen

Latisha. The name suited her. I tried to keep her name at the forefront of my thoughts but her hand on my cock made me lose all sense of time, space, and reality. Up and down, her strong tight hands gripped me and stroked every bump left over from my barbs being removed.

Up and down–my whole world was wrapped up in that one movement, up and down. She was going torturously slow. I looked down at her beautiful face and nearly came when I saw her confident smile. This was the Latisha I knew, not the shy woman who was so flustered by my every touch. She locked her eyes with mine and picked up the pace of her strokes.

"Gah," I gasped. I closed my eyes to try and gain some semblance of control. I wanted this to last as long as possible.

"Be a good boy and look at me, Barbarian." It was by the grace of god I didn't come right then and there.

I locked eyes with her again and watched as her lips descended upon me. I moaned as the warmth of her mouth enveloped me. She lifted her head up until all that was left in her mouth was the tip of my cock and she circled it with her wicked tongue.

"Latisha," I moaned. I felt dizzy with sensation. Her tongue on my sensitive head was pure bliss.

She went back down as low as she could and I had to remind myself to breathe. She sped up her movements as she bobbed her head up and down in rapid succession. I tried my best not to thrust into her mouth like a wild man, but then she squeezed my ass so tight I could feel every prick of her sharp nails.

I hissed and bucked into her warm mouth. Her eyes crinkled as if she were smiling but her mouth was already occupied. Her fast pace had me losing my grip on reality. I couldn't tell who I was or where I'd been. All I knew in that moment was the sensation of her lips going up and down every inch of my length. My balls felt tight and every hair on my body was standing on end in anticipation of my release.

Latisha removed one hand from my ass and started to massage my balls with it, and I could hold back no longer. Her name was on my tongue as my orgasm shot through me like a bolt of lightning radiating throughout my entire body, singeing every nerve, branding my very soul with Latisha's touch. I was hers wholly and completely.

She continued to work my shaft until I was fully wrung out. Lifting her head she gave me a wide grin. The same grin she wore on her face when she won an argument. I would pick a fight with her every day and lose just to see that grin again.

* * *

Latisha

Bowen fell to his knees before me. His chest was heaving as he struggled to catch his breath. Hearing him say my name, my real name, as I'd wrung every last drop of seed from him was a memory I'd carry with me for many years to come. I could keep my emotional distance from Bowen while I also collected memories of my time here serving in Kach's house. There wasn't any harm in that.

"Wooooo boy, I can't say I've ever felt such pleasure in all of my days." Bowen got up from the floor and sat next to me on the bed.

"Does that mean I am good at the benefits?" I wanted to hear him compliment me again.

"Come again?" His brows furrowed in confusion.

"We are friends with benefits and I just gave you the benefit," I clarified.

"Oh yes, yes you did." He laughed and then sighed with contentment. "You are very good at the benefits Latisha."

Hearing him say my name in his strange accent made me feel warm inside. It wasn't a lustful feeling. It was more like a hug. There was a rightness to it, like he should have been calling me by my real name this whole time. Bowen laid down on the bed with his hands behind his head. His biceps bulged in that position and it reminded me of how tightly he held me when we first kissed. My gaze shifted downward to his strong chest that rose and fell with each breath. He didn't have defined abs but I liked that. His stomach looked soft and inviting and I had the sudden urge to lay down upon it.

I shifted my vision downward to gaze upon his studded cock. I wanted him inside of me again. As soon as the thought crossed my mind a purring started to rumble in my chest.

"Now that's a sound that's never going to get old."

As if called forth to duty, his flaccid cock hardened before my very eyes. My sex throbbed and every part of me felt overly sensitive. I needed Bowen and I needed him now. But how would we do this? I knew I wasn't brave enough to mate with him face-to-face, but even bent over the bed Bowen was making me feel emotions that scared me. Not seeing any other way to go, I decided I would just have to shove my emotions down.

"I'd like to bend over the bed again, but I still don't want you to touch me. That's still my boundary."

Bowen stood with his hands on his hips and frowned down at me.

"Latisha, we've been over this."

"We didn't exactly finish our discussion from earlier. I told you my boundary and you disagreed with me." I crossed my arms over my chest.

"Why? Why is no touching your boundary?"

"Because...because it's too much." I didn't mean

to be honest with Bowen, but the words spilled out of my mouth before I could stop them. His gaze softened and for once he looked like he didn't know what to say.

I sighed and sat down on the bed. "I may be throbbing with the need to mate, but that doesn't mean I'm ready for intimacy. I need this to be clinical. I need you to just be a friend with benefits and nothing more." I looked up into his swirling green eyes and pleaded, "Please."

Bowen solemnly nodded. "I understand."

I sighed with relief. A part of me was disappointed that Bowen didn't argue further, I wanted to see his face when he came and I wanted him to see mine, but a much bigger part of me knew this was just the way it had to be. The walls guarding my emotions were already weak enough. Any weaker and I might just admit that I liked Bowen, *really* liked him, and I couldn't have that; not now, not ever.

I took off my dress and bent over the bed and waited for Bowen to approach me. He didn't move and silence filled the room. I was about to turn and say something witty, something mean perhaps, but then I heard footsteps as he approached the bed. He stood behind me and I could feel his warmth on my back. A shiver of anticipation ran down my spine.

"Are you alright there, sweetheart?" His voice was raspy with a hint of sadness like he knew I wanted more than this.

"I'm fine," I whispered. "I'm also lubricated so we can just get started. We do not need your 'foreplay'." My voice was firmer this time. Firm enough for even me to believe what I was saying.

"Right, clinical," he sighed.

He stepped even closer and placed a firm hand on each hip. My purring got even louder and I already felt weak in the knees. There was something about Bowen's touch that was more intense than any of the other males' I had mated with. I had never been so thoroughly affected by anyone like this before. I scratched the base of my horns and placed my hand back down on the bed.

Bowen slid his cock through my sex and covered himself in my essence. I was so sensitive that even that movement sent pleasure rippling through me. A moan escaped my lips and I was ready to beg for more.

"Are you ready, Latisha?" *Latisha.* My name came out as a purr.

"Yes," I breathed.

He took a hand off my hip and used it to guide himself to my entrance. He sank into me and we moaned in unison as my sex surrounded his shaft. Every bump that passed through me made my channel flutter with small waves of pleasure.

With both hands firmly on my hips again he held me in place as he slowly eased out of me and slowly eased back in.

"Perfect, so perfect," he whispered under his breath.

He set a torturously slow pace shifting in and out of me. Heat pooled in my core as my climax slowly billowed to the surface.

I felt his hand caressing my back. His fingers ran over every inch of my spine and his thumb grazed the column of my neck. His touch was soft and gentle and it made my heart ache. I wanted his touch, maybe even more than I wanted him inside me. Bowen saw all of me, the good and the bad. I wanted to get to know him, I wanted him to hold me, I wanted...I needed him to stop.

"No touching," my tone came out harsher than I had wanted but it did the trick.

"Oh, sorry, I hadn't realized." He removed his hand from my back and placed it on my hip once again.

His slow pace sped up and I moved my hips to meet his every thrust. He moaned as I moved in time with him and I felt that moan all the way to my core. I was overwhelmed with sensation. Every muscle in my body felt tight, ready for release, and despite every glorious undulation of Bowen's hips positioning his studded shaft into my channel I needed more.

"Bo–Barbarian, I need...I need..." I couldn't form words anymore. I couldn't think past the cock entering and leaving my body over and over again, each time better than the last.

"You need more, sweetheart?" His words came out as grunts through gritted teeth.

"Yes," I whined.

"Can I touch you here?" He cupped my sex and even that small amount of friction on my perilla drew a guttural sound of pleasure from my lips.

"You have to say it, Latisha. Say that you want

me to touch you."

"I...I want to come. Please," I begged. I wouldn't admit that I needed his touch. I couldn't, I wanted it too much. Saying it outloud might break something in me that I wasn't ready to be broken.

"Close enough," he grunted.

I felt his finger circle my sensitive flesh and my hips bucked involuntarily. Every sensation suddenly became heightened as that one finger circled me over and over again. Every bump on his shaft felt larger, every stroke felt deeper, every breath of his I felt on my back felt sweeter.

Everything was rising in a crescendo: larger, harder, deeper, sweeter until that one finger flicked back and forth over my flesh and I came undone.

My back locked into place as my channel spasmed, sending a flood of pleasure with it from my horns to my toes.

Bowen cried out his own pleasure, his hands gripping me tight, as he finished with a few final strokes. My legs trembled and I was more than happy to sit on the bed as soon as he pulled out of me.

Bowen collapsed on the bed as well. "You're incredible Latisha, every bit of you."

"What did I say about complimenting me?"

"You said I couldn't compliment you during sex, not afterward," he rebutted.

"Fine, you win," I conceded.

Bowen looked thoughtful. "I don't want to win, Latisha. I've never wanted to win."

There was no way that could be true. "Then

why are you always arguing with me if you don't want to win?"

"I just want to talk to you and arguing seems to be the best way to do it." Bowen gave me a sheepish smile as if he'd just tattled on himself.

I took his hand in mine. "Never stop, Bowen. Never stop arguing with me." I wasn't ready for intimacy yet, but if I ever was ready, I wanted to be with Bowen and no one else.

"Never," he smiled.

CHAPTER 17

Bowen

I pulled on my pants as Latisha got up to eat more fruit and cheese. Her sweet pussy had a vice grip on my soul, that was for damn sure. God, any doubt that my body recognized Latisha as my mate was gone now. The sex was good even without caressing her like I wanted to.

It had made me stop short when she confessed she wasn't ready for intimacy. I should have figured that. She had some deep wounds that weren't going to heal until she was ready, but I could be patient. As long as she was working here I had a chance to win her over, a chance to convince her to let me into her heart.

"That was quite good... for a Barbarian." I sat up and saw Latisha pulling on her dress and smiling at me. I knew I had left her satisfied; she was just toying with me. "I was starting to question if you'd be any good after seeing your strange dancing at the after-party," she added.

"You want to see talent? Come here and I'll show you talent." I helped her to her feet and drew her in close to me. I put my hand on the small of her back and took her hand and held it up and to the side as if we were about to waltz around the room.

"We've danced together before, Barbarian, this isn't new." Despite her protest, she let me lead her in slow circles around the room.

"Yes, but that was a brief dance and the music was no good." I took a deep breath and started counting out our steps as I led her in a country waltz.

"1-2-3-4, 1-2-3-4, 1-2-3-4." I let my voice die out in a whisper. "I don't know many songs, and I'm not the best singer, but one song comes to mind when I think of you."

"Oh yeah? I'd like to hear one of your Earth songs."

I took a deep breath and prayed Latisha wouldn't laugh at my voice. "You are my sunshine, my only sunshine," Latisha giggled as I sang.

I stopped mid-lyric. "You don't like my song?"

"I just find it funny that someone can be another person's sunshine."

"It makes sense to me. I know my day gets brighter every time I see you." Her cheeks flushed a dark blue and she looked down at her feet. I smiled at her shyness and I started up my song again.

"You are my sunshine, my only sunshine. You make me happy when skies are gray. You'll never know dear how much I love you, so please don't take my sunshine away."

She and I circled the room as I sang. Latisha looked down at our feet while I stared at her, mesmerized by her pointy blue ears, her long white hair, and how the corner of her mouth turned up just slightly when she was pleased but didn't want anyone to know it.

"This is a short song."

"Well there's more to it, but it's too sad to sing."

"I like sad songs. Will you sing it for me?"

"Of course, your wish is my command." That phrase had brought a smile to her face before, and she was smiling again now. I just knew when she was comfortable and ready for intimacy she would be commanding me to do all kinds of things in the bedroom. My dick hardened and pressed painfully against my pants at the mere thought of it.

I took a deep breath and started the second half of the song. "*The other night dear while I lay sleeping. I dreamt I held you in my arms, but when I woke I was mistaken and I hung my head and I cried.*"

"Your sunshine song is really about someone who lost the one that they loved?"

"I'm afraid so."

"That *is* sad."

The song had me thinking about what it would be like when Latisha left Kach's house forever, and my heart nearly stopped beating in my chest. I knew this was only an intel job for her. She wasn't really a servant and she probably didn't even need the money. As talented as she was she had to be getting paid a pretty penny by her real employer, whoever that may be.

"People don't usually sing that half of the song. In fact, most people on my homeworld have forgotten about it altogether."

"I like your sunshine song. Will you sing the first half again?" Latisha looked up at me with her piercing gray eyes.

"Of course." I moved my hands to her hips and she put her hands on my shoulders. We slow-danced around the room while I sang and Latisha rested her head on my chest.

* * *

Latisha

Bowen stopped singing his song and suddenly we were standing in the middle of the room just holding each other. I looked into his green eyes and laughed at his twitching ears.

"What's so funny?"

"Your ears twitch when you're nervous or agitated."

He swallowed hard. "Oh, yeah." His cheeks turned pink and he looked away. "I suppose that's true."

I ran a finger along a pink cheek. "Do I make you nervous or agitated?"

"Both," He grinned a wide toothy grin and I laughed again.

I could stay in this moment forever. I liked being held by Bowen, there was a rightness to it. On the few occasions a male has chosen to hold me an overwhelming urge to run had always come over me, but I didn't feel that with Bowen. I felt content and at peace.

He stroked my back in a way that I was quickly becoming addicted to. His fingers ran up and down my spine, reaching the base of my tail. His touch sent ripples of pleasure straight to my core and I started to purr. My third and final rut of the day was here.

"Music to my ears," Bowen commented with a knowing smile on his face.

We both tried to take a step forward at the same time and ended up tripping over each other and falling on the bed. I landed on my back and Bowen landed on top of me.

My purring grew even louder and before I could even think about what I was doing I pulled Bowen down on top of me and kissed him. He moaned as soon as our lips touched. I teased the seam of his lips and deepened the kiss as soon as he parted for me. Our tongues explored each other's mouths and I wanted more. I ground my hips against his hard shaft and moaned at the delightful friction.

Bowen hissed, clearly as pleased by my gyrations as I was.

I wanted more though. I wanted to kiss, to hold, to grind and to mate face-to-face. I wanted to look into Bowen's eyes as he sank into me and, for the first time in my life, feel beautiful during a mating. I wanted to let my guard down and let him in, not just my body but my heart too.

I'd never wanted that before, and that scared me. I was so close to betraying the oath I'd made to myself to never let anyone close to me again. I couldn't trust anyone. I couldn't let anyone in. If my own mother could betray me then Bowen could too. That was just a fact of life. I didn't want to know what that kind of heartbreak would feel like. I didn't want to be crushed under the weight of the loss of his love.

"Stop," I commanded, and Bowen froze.

I wiggled out from under him and searched for my apron. "I have to go." I picked my apron and bandana up off the floor and headed for the door.

"Latisha, stop! Just talk to me. If I've wronged you in any way give me a chance to make it right," he pleaded.

My hand was already on the doorknob. "You didn't do anything wrong. I just have to go."

Bowen put his hand on the door to block me from opening it. "You still have one rut left."

"And what? I should spend it with you, Barbarian?"

Pain flashed on his face and I knew I had hurt him. Good. Better I hurt him than he hurt me. Everyone betrays everyone in the end.

"That's not what I was saying." He sighed and stepped away from the door. "If you truly want to go then go, but if you just want to be alone then I'll be the one to leave."

He picked up his belt and shirt and headed for the door. "You don't need to spend your final rut laying in a bed with ten other women in the same room."

"I..." I didn't know what to say. Damn him for being impossibly kind when I'd been illogically mean.

"It was a pleasure being with you today, Latisha." He opened the door and paused. "I know I don't have any place to say this, but if you…if you ever choose to take another lover make sure they treat you right. You're beautiful, a goddess, and you deserve to be treated as such."

He left the room and gently closed the door, leaving me alone with a tray of food and a heavy heart. I leaned my forehead against the wood and prayed to the goddess for Bowen to return. I'd never felt so hollow in my life.

"Come back, come back, come back," I whispered, but he was gone. I'd asked for space and he'd given it to me.

I sat on the bed and pressed my transmitter pendant until the black stone turned red. I needed to think about something else, anything else. I updated Jaris on everything that was going on. He responded via my buzzpad, letting me know he was going to pay Kach a visit soon and to be ready.

I could do that. I would love to do that actually. I would love to do anything other than think about how alone I felt in this empty room.

CHAPTER 18

Bowen

"Good evening, Jaris. Monstair Kach is waiting for you in the study."

"Tha-Thank you, Venpan." A tall lean Sirret man entered the mortress. I'd been told he was one of Kach's closest friends. Gunok said this Jaris was the son of a merchant, but I didn't know if I believed that. He certainly didn't act like any of the merchants I'd met. Merchants carried themselves with a haughty arrogance. This man had none of that. He was more humble, more approachable.

"How have you been, Venpan? I haven't seen you for a while." A merchant asking a servant how they'd been? This man truly was different from the rest.

"I've been well. Thank you for asking." They continued to weave down the hallway to the study, and I, the obedient bodyguard, followed them. When they arrived at the study, my breath caught as I laid eyes on Latisha. She was standing on her tippy-toes, stretching to dust a light fixture that was located well above her head.

Seeing her stretched out like that made me feel

things I'd been trying to suppress ever since I left Latisha last night. Walking away from her was the hardest thing I'd ever had to do in my life, but there was no way around it. I couldn't force Latisha to let me in, no matter how much I wanted her, and no matter how much she wanted me, it wouldn't happen until she was ready. I just wished that I could go back in time and protect her from every person who'd wounded her, every person who'd broken her trust. I would do it all just for the chance that she might trust me, and maybe even accept me as her mate.

"Jaris, old friend! It's great to see you!" Kach opened the door and greeted his fellow merchant.

"Thank you for having me." Jaris gave Kach a small bow.

"Come, walk with me. I want to show you the updates I've made to the mortress since you were last here."

My master and his guest started down the hallway. Venpan attempted to follow them holding a tray of drinks, when Latisha stepped in front of him.

"I've got this. I know you've got better things to do." Latisha gave him an innocent smile.

"Oh, thank you." Vepan handed her the tray and walked back down the hallway.

Latisha walked with broad strides to catch up with Kach and Jaris. What was she up to?

"And what about raising the wages of the laborers who work in your mine? Have you made progress on that?" Jaris had his hands clasped behind his back as he walked and chatted with Kach.

"Oh, you know how much I've been wanting to raise their wages, but my request is all tied up in bureaucracy. There are so many rules and regulations about raising wages, it just takes time."

"And yet there are no rules about lowering wages," Jaris mumbled.

Latisha's brows were drawn together as she listened intently to their conversation.

"How generous of you to carry this tray of drinks for Venpan," I whispered. I couldn't help myself. I wanted to talk to her and the best way to do that was to get her agitated enough to argue with me.

"I can be generous sometimes."

"Oh, I don't doubt it. It's just interesting that your generosity led you to be in earshot of Kach and his visitor, is all."

She frowned and her tail lashed behind her. "I can't talk right now."

"You can't talk? Is that because you have to listen to their conversation?"

Latisha finally looked at me instead of straight ahead and scowled. The corner of my mouth turned up in a grin. That was all I really wanted: was to see her scowl at me as if nothing had changed between us. As if she hadn't shut me out last night. Her eyes drifted to my lips and her face softened.

"What about you and that mate of yours? I still can't believe that I dropped you off as a single male in need of a rut specialist, and you came out of that resort having found your true mate." Kach slapped the back of Jaris' shoulder and laughed.

"I can hardly believe it myself most days. Anna is a dream come true. I wish I could be with her right now."

"Well, don't let me hold you back," Kach laughed.

"Oh, sorry old friend. I didn't mean it like that." Jaris's shoulders slumped in embarrassment.

"Don't worry about it. If I had a mate, I'd want to be spending all my time with her as well." A brief silence drifted between them. "Speaking of your mate, where is that safe house of yours? You know I worry when I can't reach you."

"It wouldn't be a safe house if everyone knew its location, Kach." Jaris elbowed him.

"Right you are my friend, right you are."

Kach opened the doors to the parlor room, turned and grabbed two drinks off of Latisha's tray, and shut the door behind them.

Before I could say another word Latisha was already halfway down the hallway. I had to suppress the urge to follow her and stay at my post. I'd catch up with her later, I promised myself.

* * *

Latisha
CW: attempted sexual assult

Why did Bowen have to be on duty at the house today? Being around him made me dizzy with emotions. I was both elated to see him and sad about the way things had ended last night. I wanted to run right up to him and hold him and feel him hold me. But I couldn't. So instead I was my grumpy self and Bowen loved it, which made me feel so much worse. *Come on Latisha, focus.* Jaris was here, and I needed to be ready for anything.

Things were going well, I reminded myself. Jaris was with Kach, hopefully having a productive conversation. I still needed to provide backup in case anything went wrong, so I headed up one floor to the linen closet. The air vent was directly above the parlor room, and I could hear every word they spoke if I put my ear down to it.

"I can't do that Kach. It's just not right." Jaris sounded distressed.

"It's for their own good. If this rebellion continues they're just going to get hurt. You think the rival houses are going to just stand by and watch while the rebellion attacks them? There are just two houses left, mine and Dirgach. Think what will happen if all the other rival houses got together to mount an attack. I just want to protect the laborers. With you by my side, we'll be a united front. They'll listen to you." Kach sounded surprisingly sincere.

"No, I won't stand in the way of the rebellion. They might get hurt, but that is their choice to make. I will not ask them to stand down."

"I understand, but I had to ask," Kach sighed. "Here, have another drink." There was a pause before Kach continued. "To friendship."

"To friendship," Jaris replied.

A moment later I heard a loud thump like something heavy hit the floor.

The parlor room door creaked open and I heard Kach say, "My friend has collapsed."

"Do you want me to call for a medic, Monstair," Bowen's voice came through the air vent.

"No, I think he just had too much to drink. Take him to the guest room and lay him on the bed." Kach sounded very calm for a person who just witnessed their best friend pass out in front of them.

"Yes, Monstair Kach."

Bif me. Jaris couldn't have passed out from just two drinks. What was going on?

I made my way up another floor to the guest room and hid in the shadows as Bowen carried Jaris' limp body into the room. A moment later Kach and Bowen were stepping into the hallway.

"Guard this door. Make sure no one gets in or out." Again Kach looked unphased by the situation.

"Or out?" Bowen questioned.

"Yes, I'm afraid our guest might not be feeling well and really shouldn't be on his feet."

"I see."

"Good kitty," Kach patted Bowen on the arm and walked away.

I had to suppress the urge to chase after him and demand he treat Bowen with respect.

I needed to remain calm and to come up with a plan to get to Jaris. This would actually be easier if it were any of the other guards standing outside that room. I could easily surprise and overtake any of them, but I knew Bowen would sniff me out in a heartbeat. His senses seemed to be more acute than a Sirriet's.

I would have to try to talk my way into that room. I bit back a sigh. I could do this. I could be my usual not-charming self and convince him to let me in. I strode up to the door and stopped in front of the male who made my heart flutter every time I saw him.

"Hello, how may I help you, Ms. Layla." He had an unbearably handsome smirk on his face. I hated that he used my alias. It made sense. He couldn't use my real name out in the open like this, but it still grated on me when I longed to hear my real name in his smooth voice.

"I need to get in that room." Why lie? He would figure it out eventually and telling the truth might get me to Jaris faster.

"Now, why would I let you do that?" Bowen crossed his arms over his chest.

"I know him."

He lifted an eyebrow. "You're going to have to do better than that."

I ran a hand down my face and sighed. "I work for him."

Bowen smiled, "I told you I'd get you to tell me your secrets one day."

"Are you going to unlock the door or not?" I huffed.

"No." His gaze was locked on me, challenging me to defy him.

"Barbarian, please." I didn't have time for this.

"I'm not unlocking this door until you do two things. One, tell me what your real job is, and two, say please one more time. I like to hear you say it." His last request came out as a purr.

"Just those two things?" I did not hold back the sarcasm in my tone.

"A kiss wouldn't hurt, but only if you want to. It's no fun otherwise."

My tail thumped on the floor. I'd like to kiss him again. The thought of his lips on mine made my skin heat and brought back all the memories from yesterday.

"I'm not kissing you." I bit out and crossed my arms.

"I didn't think you would." Bowen crossed his arms over his chest as well. I felt his tail wrap around my ankle. It must have been an unconscious movement on his part. He didn't look down or acknowledge it. I didn't have it in me to shake his tail off me. Whether he was doing it consciously or unconsciously I enjoyed his touch.

"Go on, spill the beans." He gestured toward me.

"That wasn't part of our agreement. I have no beans to spill." Why was he adding this strange request to his list of demands?

He grinned. "Tell me your secrets, woman."

"I am not a woman. I am a Sirret Female." I knew what he meant, but I couldn't help myself. If I couldn't kiss him I would have to settle for arguing with him.

"You are a goddess, but I'm still not letting you in until you've done what I've asked."

"You are insufferable."

"I've been called worse," he smirked.

"Fine. Jaris runs a security company and I work on his team."

He made a circular motion with his hand encouraging me to continue.

"He tasked me with getting intel on the rebellion and how Kach might be connected to it. Now are you going to open that door?"

"Are you going to say please?"

"Please unlock the door." I put my hands on my hips.

"That's a good girl." Warmth pooled at my core. Being his good girl sounded nice but I thought being his bad girl would be even better.

He typed in the key code and we both filed into the guest room. Jaris was laying on his back breathing in and out deeply.

"Jaris." I gently shook his shoulder. "Jaris, wake up." I shook his shoulder a bit harder. He didn't stir.

"That's not good." Bowen approached the bedside and gently lifted Jaris' eyelids.

"What are you doing?"

"I'm not really sure. When humans are drunk their pupils are slow to dilate, but his got smaller right away in response to the light in the room. I don't know much about Sirret biology but I think it's a good sign that his eyes are responsive, but I also think that means he's not drunk."

"What happened in that room?" I wondered aloud.

"Were you listening in?"

"Of course I was listening in," I huffed, annoyed that Bowen knew exactly who I was now and what I did. I felt emotionally naked around him and that feeling was both uncomfortable and pleasant. It had been a long time since I was around someone who knew me so thoroughly. Even Jaris only knew me professionally. He didn't know me on a personal level like Bowen did.

"We need to get him out of here," his voice brought me out of my thoughts. "There's something off about his relationship with Kach. I don't think he's safe in this house."

"Jaris has a safehouse not too far from here that I can take him to." There was a large apartment just two blocks from here that I had the keycode to. Jaris had about five safe houses in the city just in case anyone on his team needed to escape from a sticky situation.

"*We* will take him to the safe house, not just you." Bowen had his arms crossed over his chest and his ears twitched.

"I didn't ask for your help." I crossed my arms to match Bowen's stance.

"And I didn't ask for your permission. I'm helping you whether you like it or not."

"You are so irritating." My tail thumped on the floor. Why couldn't he just let me handle things on my own? He was like a sexy shadow that I couldn't run away from.

"And you're stubborn as a mule," he frowned.

My resolve cracked under his gaze. I guess there were worse things in life than Bowen helping me carry Jaris a few blocks away from the house.

"Fine, let's get going before Kach comes back."

Bowen picked up Jaris' limp body and placed it over his shoulder. "Are you going to tell me the location of this safehouse or is that a secret, too?"

"It's a few blocks away, behind a fancy clothing shop. Now you stay here and I'll check to see if the hallway is clear."

"Yes, ma'am," Bowen purred. His tone sent a pleasurable shiver down my spine.

I looked both ways down the hallway. It was empty.

"It's clear. I'm going to check the stairwell."

Bowen walked behind me carrying Jaris and I quickly made my way down the stairs. If we ran into anyone I wanted to be well ahead of Bowen so I could distract them somehow.

Three flights of stairs later, things were looking good. The last flight of stairs was connected to a short hallway. There was no one in the corridor, so I pushed the door open to the small stairwell and found myself face to face with Cruun and Gunok, the last two people I wanted to see tonight.

"Look Cruun, the goddess has blessed us with a treat tonight." Gunok smiled and took a puff of his fume stick. This stairwell was dimly lit with only one small light still working.

"I'm not here for you." I turned to go back out into the hallway when Gunok grabbed my arm and slammed me against the wall.

"The fact that you're so prickly is going to make it all the sweeter when I sink into you." My blood went cold.

Cruun untied my apron and tugged it away from my body. Then Gunok reached up my dress and toyed with the waistband of my underwear. I tried wiggling my arm free but Gunok's grasp was too tight. I waited for him to bring his head closer to me so I could damage him with my horns but he was too aware of a move like that to let himself get close.

"Take off her underwear. I'll hold her here so she can't do any damage."

Cruun walked over and got on his knees. Just as he reached for the waistband I kneed him in the face.

"Bif you!" He fell back holding a hand over his eye.

I yanked my arm down as hard as I could but Gunok's grip was still too tight. Cruun got back up on his feet and stalked toward me.

"I'm going to make you pay for that."

In the darkness, I saw movement behind the guards. Was that Bowen?

One moment it was just Cruun, Gunok, and I in the stairwell, the next Bowen was there holding a knife to each male's throat. I felt his tail wrap around my leg, the small gesture was immensely comforting. Bowen was here and I knew I was safe.

"I suggest you take your hands off her." Bowen's

face was contorted into a snarl.

"Why?" Gunok grunted. "What does she mean to you?"

"Keep touching her and find out. Go ahead, I've been itching for another fight and you're just my size."

"It's not worth it Gunok," Cruun insisted. "You heard what he did to that Sirret. He sliced the end of his tail right off." Gunok nodded and put his hands in the air. Cruun followed suit. The males ran out of the stairwell as soon as Bowen released them.

As soon as they left I pulled up my underwear and picked up my apron off the floor.

"The stairwell is clear." I smiled at Bowen trying to hide how shaken I felt by the situation.

Bowen didn't buy it. He cupped my cheek in his hand and pulled me in for a hug. I melted into him. I needed this, and as much as I tried to fight it, I had to admit I felt safe with Bowen, felt protected. Could I learn to let him protect me? Would I ever be able to let my guard down enough to lean on him for support and trust that he wouldn't betray me? Hadn't he earned that? I genuinely didn't know. Pushing people away had become second nature to me. It was as much a part of me as my leg or my tail. Could I really let that go?

All of these questions would have to wait. Bowen released me and placed Jaris back over his shoulder.

"It's probably best if we get going." He tried to smile but there was no joy on his face.

"Yeah." We exited the mortress and headed out

into the night.

It wasn't long before we reached the safehouse. I typed in the code and sighed with relief as we walked in and the door slid closed behind us.

CHAPTER 19

Bowen

Deep breaths in and out. I was still trying to calm my nerves after seeing Latisha pinned against the wall with Cruun and Gunok licking their lips like she was nothing more than a piece of meat. That vision would haunt my dreams for the rest of my days. Even now I could barely contain the urge to wrap Latisha in my arms just to remind myself that she was safe.

Jaris was laying on the bed but he was still unresponsive.

"Was it just wine in those glasses you served them?" I asked Latisha as she typed something out on her buzzpad.

"It smelled like regular wine to me. Why?"

"I think one of those glasses had wine and the other had a sleeping drug of some kind."

Latisha looked over at Jaris and nodded as she processed the information.

"Kach did act very casual about the whole thing."

Holocall from Anna Hart, a robotic voice interrupted our conversation.

"That would be his mate. I alerted her that something had happened to Jaris." Latisha walked over to the wall and pressed the button to receive the call.

"Latisha, it's good to see you. You said that Jaris was in trouble?" An image of a human woman with creamy skin was projected onto the wall. She worried her bottom lip as she waited for Latisha's reply.

"Yes, unfortunately, I think he's been drugged. He's unconscious, but otherwise seems fine."

"Drugged?! By who?" The color drained from Anna's face.

"We think Kach, but there's a small chance it could have been someone else."

"Why would Kach do this?" Anna started to bite her nails.

"I'm still working on that. I'll get back to you as soon as I have more information." Latisha was calm and measured as she delivered the information. Her calm demeanor helped keep Anna calm as well. She stopped biting her nails and stood up straight.

"I'll fill Maggie and Claire in on what's going on, then I'll be on my way to Ozinda." Anna was looking more confident now that she had a plan.

Latisha gave her a solemn nod before Anna cut off the call.

"It's going to be a few day cycles before she gets there. I want to get Jaris some medicine to counteract whatever drug he was given before she gets here."

"I know someone who might have the medicine he needs. I can go get it for him." I offered. I was sure Krix would have something.

The tension in Latisha's shoulders eased a little. "Thank you. That would be helpful."

I started to walk down the stairs to leave the house when I turned back around. "Don't let anyone in unless it's me."

Latisha rolled her eyes. "This isn't my first security job, Barbarian. I know what I'm doing."

"All the same, it'll make me feel more at ease if you gave me your word." I thought for a moment before I continued. "Here I'll show you my special knock."

I walked to the wall and did a *rat-a-tat-tat* knock.

Latisha put her hands on her hips, "You're being ridiculous."

"Dammit woman, just say yes," I huffed in an exasperated tone.

"Fine, yes. I won't open the door unless I hear your silly knock."

"Thank you," I sighed with relief. After the night we'd had I didn't want to take any chances. I knew Latisha was capable, but still, a man could only take so much.

I returned an hour later with medicine that Krix promised would counteract almost any sleeping agent. Krager was once again not happy that I'd woken up her wife in the wee hours of the morning, but once I explained the situation, they were both sympathetic to Jaris' plight. She did warn me, however, that I was becoming her least favorite customer.

I did the special knock that I had shown Latisha earlier and waited for her to answer. When I didn't hear any footsteps coming toward the door, I entered the keycode I had watched Latisha enter earlier and snuck into the house. I was immediately greeted with an unfamiliar male scent that set me on edge.

I crept up the stairs and peered around the corner to the bedroom Jaris was laying in. Latisha sat on the edge of the bed and looked calm. Sitting across from her on a chair was a large winged Vorst. This woman was so damn infuriating. She couldn't have waited an hour for me to get back?

"Thank you for coming, Gullex. I really appreciate you looking after Jaris until his mate arrives."

"It is nothing, less than losing an old feather off my wing," the large male smiled.

"You couldn't have waited for me to get back," I announced my return.

Gullex stood up, muscles tensed for a fight. Clearly neither one of them had heard my approach.

"We need to get back to the mortress and Gullex agreed to look after Jaris so we could do so." Latisha gestured to the Vorst.

Gullex relaxed upon realizing that I was a friend and not a foe.

"Can we trust him?" I gestured to Gullex as well.

"Yes," she sighed. "Drannon, my teammate, vouched for him.

I looked him up and down. He really was huge,

by far one of the tallest and broadest beings I'd seen on Ozinda.

"Alright then," I nodded.

"I wasn't asking for your approval." Latisha rolled her eyes. "Do you have the medicine?"

"Yes, I do." I handed her the medicated patch Krix gave me and she promptly removed it from the packaging and placed it on Jaris' arm.

"Krix said it would be a few hours before it took full effect," I added.

"Okay," Latisha nodded and sighed. "Thank you again Gullex, I'll check back in with you tomorrow."

We walked down the stairs and exited the house.

"I would appreciate it if you would answer the door next time," I tried to sound annoyed, but I knew better than anyone that Latisha was not one to wait around.

"I was busy," was her nonchalant reply.

"I see that." I held out my hand for her and my heart soared when she took it.

CHAPTER 20

Latisha

I enjoyed walking hand in hand with Bowen. It was comfortable. It felt right. But this would be where our connection ended. This would be one of the last memories of Bowen I'd get to collect. It was clear that my time here was coming to an end. I'd be leaving Ozinda and Bowen would stay here. The penalty for running out on a servant contract was a lifetime of imprisonment. I wouldn't ask Bowen to risk that to leave with me. Besides, I still wasn't sure if I could ever let Bowen in, not in the way he wanted.

We walked to the third floor where the men's dorm was located and I thought that was where we'd part, but Bowen kept a hold of my hand and continued walking up the stairs.

"What are you doing?" I let my hand fall away from his.

"I'm walking you to the women's dorm." His tail wrapped around my leg.

"I don't need you to do that," I huffed.

"I need to do it. I need to make sure you make it there alive and well."

"Make it where? Up one flight of stairs?" I pointed to the dormitory door.

"Yes," was all he said, as if it were a decision set in stone.

"Well, don't. I don't need you. In fact, I don't *want* you. I don't want your protection or your kindness." What I needed was to push Bowen away. This would all be so much easier if I left Ozinda knowing he was upset with me. If I could push him away he might not miss me when I left.

"Damnit woman, why do you insist on making it so hard for me to take care of you?"

"Because I don't want you to!" My yell echoed through the stairwell and I winced.

"Why? Tell me why, Latisha." His ears were twitching.

"Because this is all temporary!" There it was. I'd let it slip out. I might as well keep going. "In a few day cycles I'll be leaving Ozinda and you'll be here serving Kach. What we have is going to be over, so why draw it out?"

He filled the space between us and pinned me with an intense stare. "You don't think I'd follow you to the ends of this universe, Latisha? You leave, I leave. I don't give a damn about the consequences."

"And if I asked you to not follow me, what would you do?" I needed him to stay. I wasn't brave enough to let him in.

"I'd walk as far behind you as I could so you wouldn't see me in the shadows."

"Why? Why can't you let me go? I'm mean to

you, I've pushed you away, I ended our mating early, I've given you every reason to not like me."

"Because I can't quit you. I understand you have trust issues but-"

"Yes, I do," I cut him off. "I don't trust anyone, and I never will, not even you. It's how I survive."

"No Latisha, that's how you've survived. You can make a different choice. You don't have to keep living your life this way." The implication was clear. I could choose him.

"I don't think I can do that." A tear streamed down my face and I quickly wiped it away.

"You can! I know you can!" He put both hands on my shoulders and looked as if he wanted to shake some sense into me.

Don't trust anyone, Latisha. That haunting voice rang in my ears.

"I need to go. Please don't follow me." I walked up the stairs and braved a peek down at Bowen. He was standing where I'd left him looking up at me. Hurt was written all over his face. My heart broke. I wanted to go to him. I wanted to let him in, but my feet stayed planted on the ground. I just wasn't brave enough. A part of me believed that Bowen would never hurt me, but I also remembered being a child and thinking the same thing about my mother. When given the choice she'd sat there and done nothing. My own mother had betrayed me. Frozen with indecision, I continued to walk to the women's dorm.

I laid in bed and tried not to cry. I needed a distraction, so I checked my buzzpad messages. *Thank you again for bringing Jaris to the safe house. You have no idea what that means to me. If you need anything let me know. I can bring you anything you need when I get to Ozinda.*

The sentiment in Anna's statement may have been small. All she did was offer to bring me something when she got to Ozinda, but it was the offer that broke me. Her mate was lying on a bed nearly lifeless, and here she was still taking me into consideration.

Something inside me broke. The walls I'd been trying so hard to keep up for my whole life came crashing down. I didn't want to live like this anymore. I wanted more than to just survive. Every choice I'd made since my mother's betrayal has been centered on survival, not joy, not love, not kindness–just survival.

You can make a different choice. Instead of my mother's words haunting my thoughts, it was Bowen's that came through. I could make a different choice. I could choose to *live*. I could risk heartbreak if it meant I could get the reward of friendship with Anna. I could risk betrayal if it meant I could love and be loved by Bowen.

Feeling brave, I messaged Anna back. "You're welcome. Maybe you can make me some of those Earth cookies when this is all over." It was small but it was something. I'd accepted Anna's kindness and I felt ready to give her kindness in return. My heart soared at the thought that maybe we could even be real friends one day, sharing secrets and laughs like I'd seen her do with Maggie and Claire.

But I wasn't done. I wanted to keep pushing myself. I wanted Bowen. I was done holding back. I was done with just surviving.

I ran out of the room, down the stairs, and tripped over someone as I reached for the men's door. I felt warm familiar hands gripping my waist to prevent my fall. It was Bowen. He was sitting outside the door.

His face was wet with tears. I settled myself onto his lap, and without a word, I wiped them away.

"What are you doing out of bed? Did something happen? Are you hurt?" My heart nearly broke all over again at his thoughtfulness.

"I am hurt. I'm broken, Bowen." His breath stuttered as I said his name. "I'm so broken, I've never let anyone in before, not since my mother..." I let the words trail off. He already knew the story. "But I want to make a different choice. I want to let you in."

Another tear streamed down his face and I wiped that one away too. "I can't promise I'll be very good at it. I'll probably push you away and be mean every time I feel too vulnerable, but I want to try."

His throat worked as he swallowed. "I knew you could do it." His voice was nothing but a wet whisper.

I put my hand in his and intertwined our fingers together. "I still don't understand why you like me," I laughed.

He cupped my face in his hand. "Have I ever told you how sensitive my hearing is?"

"No." I wasn't sure where he was going with

this, but I was willing to be patient to find out.

"I can hear everyone's heartbeat in every room I'm in." He ran his thumb up and down my cheek and I leaned into his touch. "You know what your heartbeat sounds like?" He took our conjoined hands and flattened my palm against my chest as he pressed his hand on top of mine. "Bump-da-bump-da-bump. Well right now it's beating much faster," he smiled. "Your heart beats faster every time you catch sight of me in a room, every time I walk toward you, and every time we touch, dump-da-bump-da-bump, your heart always beats faster for me. So no matter how mean you were to me, or how much you pushed me away, I knew the truth," He smiled. "And you want to know what I like about you, Latisha?"

I nodded my head.

"Everything. Every smile and every thorn. You're strong, and smart, and talented, and you don't take shit from anybody, not even me." His grin stretched wide across his face.

"I don't know that I deserve-"

"Don't you start that. Don't you dare," he cut me off. "You've spent your whole life surviving, not trusting anyone. Of course it took you a little while to learn to let someone in, and let me tell ya, you are worth the wait every second of it, sweetheart."

We sat there for a moment breathing each other in. The silence was comfortable between us as we let this moment sink into our souls.

I stood up from Bowen's lap and held out my hand. "Come on."

He took my hand in his. "Where are we going?"

"The spare room. I'd like to finish what we started," I winked.

He let out a hearty laugh, the most joyous sound to ever reach my ears, and scooped me up into his arms as he bounded up the stairs.

We entered the spare room and I locked the door behind us. By the time I turned around, Bowen already had his shirt off. I giggled at his eagerness. I felt the same way. I joined him in shedding my clothes and bandana and soon enough we stood there naked with our garments piled on top of each other on the floor.

I looked down and he was already hard. I longed to have his studded cock inside me again. I longed to be touched by him, to take our time, to be... intimate for the first time in my life.

He stalked toward me until we were face to face. Then he placed his hand on the small of my back and pushed me even closer to him. The heat of his bare skin on mine sent a thrill through me.

He swallowed hard and trailed his thumb over my lower lip. "Are you sure you want this? We can wait if you want to."

I took his thumb into my mouth and sucked hard. He understood my answer well enough. I tilted my head up and his lips met mine with all the eagerness that had been built up inside him since the day we met. Our tongues danced on top of each other and I sucked his lower lip into my mouth which sent him into a frenzy.

He picked me up and placed me on the bed. He hovered over me and searched my face for any signs of reservation. "Can I touch you this time?"

I nodded my head. "Touch me everywhere, every inch of me is yours."

He shook his head. "I am yours. You are my goddess and I am your fool."

"Then begin your worship. This goddess doesn't have all day," I winked at him.

He barked out a laugh and leaned down. I readied myself for another kiss, but instead, his lips trailed a path from my neck to my navel. Every touch was tender, and every caress of his hands was reverent. He made his way to my sex and licked his lips as he pushed my tight curls out of the way.

He laved me from top to bottom and moaned as he tasted my essence. I squirmed under his touch, needing more. I longed for him to touch my perilla again. It was throbbing and needed his attention.

"Bowen, please," I whined.

"Say my name again. Command me to fulfill your every desire." My core clenched at his words.

"Bowen," I breathed. "Lick my perilla."

"Yes, my goddess." He dragged his tongue over my sensitive bundle of nerves and I gasped his name as my hips lifted off the bed. He drew a pattern with his tongue over and over again until my legs trembled. Then he inserted a finger in my channel and stroked me with an incredible back-and-forth motion. I was gasping for air and panting his name, but I still needed more. Pleasure radiated throughout my entire body, but not enough was focused on my core, which was aching for release.

"More," I commanded, and Bowen gave me more. He switched from licking my perilla to sucking on it, all while stroking my core and pinching my peaked nipples.

My body went taught and I cried out as the pleasure that had been radiating out, now cascaded to one central point. My channel spasmed over and over again, releasing new waves of pleasure each time.

Bowen held me tight as he laid next to me and stroked my arm as I came down from my orgasm.

"I nearly came at the sight of you cresting with pleasure. You're so goddamn beautiful." I looked down and saw his cock was shiny with the precum spilling from the tip. He caught me looking at him and slowly stroked himself.

"Give me a command, my goddess. I've waited for what feels like lifetimes to know your will."

I propped myself up on my elbow and eyed him. I'd never felt in control during a mating with anyone but Bowen, and now he was giving me even more of it.

"Stroke yourself slowly."

"Yes, ma'am," he grinned.

His hand went up and down his shaft which had become slick with his own liquid. My core clenched at the thought of him being inside me, but we had all night. That would come later.

His eyes were locked on mine as he continued to stroke himself. "Let me touch you."

"Do as you wish," I purred.

He pulled my legs until they were draped over his lap right below his sack. Then he reached down and toyed with my perilla.

"Bowen," I moaned as my hips lifted off the bed at his touch. "Stroke yourself faster," I commanded.

"As you wish." He did as he was told. His hand on my sex slowed down as he concentrated on stroking himself.

His tail thumped on the bed as his pleasure started to build. I took it in my hands and stroked it. Bowen's moan was loud and guttural, and I wanted to hear more of it. I reached the base of his tail where it was the most sensitive, and stroked him at the same speed he was stroking himself.

"Gah!" His hips lifted off the bed and his face grew taut. His hand clung to my thigh as if he needed me to stay grounded.

"Faster." He did as I commanded and I sped up my motions on his tail as well. He was panting now, his head was tilted up and his neck was taut, showing every vein and muscle. My fool needed release and I wanted to give it to him. I leaned over him and dragged my tongue in a circle around his tip.

He rasped out my name as his hips lifted off the bed once last time and his spend flooded out of him. I caressed his chest as his breathing slowed down. Then he pulled me into his arms as he caught his breath and wrapped his tail around my ankle.

"My goddess," he whispered against my neck. He couldn't see it, but I was smiling. I loved his touch and I had no idea how I had resisted it for so long.

CHAPTER 21

Bowen

I felt both wrung out and overjoyed. Tasting Latisha on my tongue and feeling her hand on my tail as I stroked myself to completion was more than I had ever hoped to have with her. I knew she could be a fierce goddess in bed.

I was so damned proud of her. I knew it couldn't have been easy to make that choice, but she'd found the courage to do it, to let her walls down and let trust in.

My breathing slowed and I lay contentedly in bed caressing Latisha's back when I felt her hand tug on my cock.

"I want you hard for me again." How could I resist a command like that? My dick stood at attention for my goddess. I was at her disposal to use me as she pleased.

"Good boy," she gave me a rough tug and I gasped at the pleasure of it.

"What would you have me do, my goddess?" Precum was already dripping from my cock with the anticipation of what she might do next.

"I want to mount you. I want to mate with you face-to-face. I want you to tell me how good it feels to be encompassed by my channel, and I want you to touch me everywhere your hands can reach." She looked at me with hooded eyes.

"You want to be intimate," I commented as I tucked her hair behind her ear.

Her eyes softened and she nodded. "I want to be intimate with you."

I sat up and caressed her lips with a soft kiss. "I'm so proud of you."

"Don't ruin this moment with all your emotions."

I barked out a laugh. Her words may have been harsh but she was smiling. There were a thousand sunsets in that smile.

I laid back down on the bed and motioned for her to come closer. She straddled me with her pussy temptingly close to my cock. She lowered herself and slid back and forth on my dick, coating me with her essence.

"Latisha," I moaned. She hadn't even mounted me yet and she felt amazing.

"Mmm," she moaned as she slid up and down my length one more time. Soon she was hovering over my shaft, and the whole word faded away as she lowered herself onto my cock. My hips thrust up involuntarily and she gasped.

"Sorry, sorry, sorry," I stroked her arms up and down as I apologized.

"You're so eager," she smiled.

"I am undone with you surrounding me," I sighed with relief.

She rolled her hips and we both moaned. "You feel so good." She commented as she rolled her hips again and again, setting a slow, sensual pace. I held tightly to her hips and reminded myself to breathe.

"Touch me, I need you closer." Her request was just above a whisper. It wasn't easy for her to ask for anything, even from me. I was going to change that, but it would take time.

I sat up and held her close to my chest. Latisha wrapped her arms and legs around me and I couldn't get over how nice it was to be embraced by the woman I had come to love. She'd come so far, and this moment was all the better for it.

I caressed her back, tracing her spine with my finger. She rocked her hips and I clung to her as pleasure rippled down every vein. When she rocked her hips again I rocked mine in time with hers.

"Yes," the word came out more as a raspy breath than anything else. "Again," she commanded, and I rocked my hips in time with hers once more. We started a slow rhythm as we held each other. She slid her fingers through my hair and kept her hand on the back of my head. I pushed her hair out of her face and saw her eyes were full of emotion.

"What does it feel like to be inside me?" she asked.

"It feels like every wish I've ever had spanning my entire lifetime all coming true at the same time." We rocked our hips again. "I spend all day with my senses being overwhelmed by everything surrounding me. The lights are too bright, the world is too noisy, every room smells bad, and even the fur on my own skin feels too hot. But when I'm inside you all of that fades away. The only thing I see is you, all I hear is your moans of pleasure, the only scent is your arousal, and the only thing I feel is the pleasure of your channel surrounding my cock. Even now I can feel you fluttering all around me. Every thrust inside you is so incredible I struggle not to come each time."

To show her how amazing she felt, I lowered my head, took her nipple into my mouth, and laved it with my tongue. Her movements stuttered and she moaned my name.

"More," she breathed. I took her other nipple into my mouth and laved that one as well. She sped up her movements and I matched mine with hers.

I grew dizzy with sensation as her channel fluttered all around me. I wrapped my tail around hers, and she tightened her tail around mine.

"I need more, Bowen."

I would give her more. I grabbed her divine ass and lifted her nearly off my cock and quickly lowered her back down again. A guttural sound escaped both our lips.

"More," she gasped.

I did it again and again until all either of us could do was hold onto each other and wait for the pleasure to take us under. Her chest had flushed a dark blue, and my balls had grown tight. I would not last much longer.

Up and down, up and down she went until Latisha cried out my name and her channel squeezed me so tight I saw stars. I held her through her orgasm and she held me through mine.

We collapsed onto the bed boneless and happy and more connected than ever.

* * *

Latisha
CW: conversation about infertility

Now *that* was an amazing sexual experience. Bowen had given me everything I could have dreamed of. His cock was amazing of course, but feeling him hold me, seeing him look into my eyes with joy, and opening myself up to intimacy was the real gift he'd given me.

He had been stroking my arm as if he couldn't stop touching me when he suddenly sat up with a shocked look on his face.

"What is it?" I looked around the room, but no one was there. I turned to face him again, and he was looking at me. "Bowen!"

"Sorry, it's just–I'm pretty sure I've memorized everything about you, and I could have *sworn* your horns were white." I could feel the color drain from my face. What was wrong with my horns? They were already broken, what else could happen to them?

"What color are they now?"

He swallowed hard. "Black." There was a long

pause as I processed the implications of his words. "Does that mean you're ill? Do you need a medic?"

I shook my head, unable to form words just yet.

"Do you know why your horns turned black?"

I nodded my head and felt tears stream down my face. This couldn't be real, could it? I'd never even considered having a mate one day, and now sitting before me was my true mate. My body had recognized him as mine and mine alone.

"Oh god, now I *know* you're sick." Bowen got up from the bed and headed for our pile of clothes. "Don't you worry. I know a good medic. She knows what she's doing and she'll fix you up right quick."

"Bowen, stop." My words sounded watery to my own ears.

He walked back to the bed and scooped me up into his arms. I turned so I could face him and cupped his face in my hands.

"You're real," I whispered. "This is really happening." I could hardly believe it.

"What's happening? Please, Latisha, I'm going crazy over here."

"You're my...my mate," I breathed.

"Of course, I'm your mate. I've known that since the day I met you."

I laughed. I should have known he'd respond like this was old information.

"No, you're my true mate, my kira-si. My body has recognized you as the one and only person for me."

"Oh." His brows drew together as he processed

what I had told him.

"Is that a good thing?" I couldn't help but ask. I was pretty sure I knew the answer but I needed to hear it out loud.

"Are you kidding? This is the best news I've received in my life!" He held me so tight I could hardly breathe. "I guess now is as good a time as any to let you know you're my true mate too."

It was my turn to be surprised. "What do you mean?"

"I mean my body recognized you as my true mate a while ago. Remember when I told you I was going through a rut?"

"Yes." He couldn't have been lying about that, his cock literally never got soft that entire day.

"Well, that was only half the truth."

"What's the other half of it?" Should I be nervous?

"Ever since I got experimented on, I couldn't get hard. For months and months, it didn't matter what I did, I couldn't get aroused; that was until I met you." That was unfortunate, but it was kind of nice knowing I was the first and only Sirret he'd ever been with.

"Ok." I waited for him to continue.

"The day after we kissed, I woke up with a hard, barbed cock. It seems that Katurso people grow barbs on their cock when they recognize their mate."

"Why didn't you tell me?"

"For what? For you to run away from me and never return?" He gave me a knowing smirk.

That was true. If he had told me he was my mate back then, I would have requested a transfer and Toran would be working this job right now.

"I'm assuming you got the barbs removed? Is that why your cock is studded now?"

"Why, yes it is." A pleased smile spread across his face.

My smile matched his. We were true mates twice over. How had I gotten so lucky? Then my smile faded.

"What's wrong? Are you upset I didn't tell you sooner?"

"Uh, no, that's fine." I worried at my bottom lip. "It's just that there's something else I haven't told you."

"Go on," Bowen's ears twitched.

"I uh, I don't have a womb so I can't have younglings."

"Ah, I see," Bowen nodded his head. "Do you want kids?" he inquired.

I shook my head no.

"Great, neither do I. Besides that, Krix thinks I'm probably infertile too." He gave me a gentle smile and squeezed my hand.

"What would you have done if I said I did want kids?" Why ask me at all if he was infertile too?

"I would have found the best-looking street kid and presented them to you as our own."

"Bowen!" I was aghast. "You can't just grab any youngling off the street and take them home!"

"You forget, you're my goddess and I'm your

fool. I'd do anything for you. There is no limit to that statement."

This male was crazy, but I already knew that. I let out a yawn. The events of this evening were starting to catch up with me.

"We should sleep. It's been a long day."

We should sleep. We were a mated pair now.

I nodded my head. Tonight we could sleep in the spare room. Someone else might need this room tomorrow, so we might as well enjoy it today.

I laid down while Bowen turned off the light and then pulled the cover up to my shoulder. He laid down next to me and pulled me into his arms.

"Promise me one thing Bowen," I whispered.

"Anything," he promised.

"Never leave me." Now that I'd allowed myself to love and be loved, now that I had my true mate, I never wanted to let him go.

"Never. You're stuck with me now. Even in the next life I'll find you and make you mine all over again."

"I'd like that," I sighed with contentment and drifted off to sleep.

CHAPTER 22

Bowen

After an incredible night of sleeping with Latisha wrapped in my arms it felt wrong to leave our little safe haven. Nonetheless, we pulled on our clothes and got ready for the day. I could imagine us in our own little house, Latisha in the closet picking out an outfit of pants and a black shirt no doubt, and me giving her a good morning kiss before I hopped into the shower. It would be domestic bliss. We'd have that one day. I'd follow her to her next job and lay low to avoid Kach and his goons. Then when the coast was clear I'd find work for myself wherever she was. Hell, I might get really lucky and Jaris would pay me to work alongside her, but if not, I could make my own way.

I looked up and Latisha was fully dressed and was draping her bandana over her horns.

"Let me get that." She lifted her hair out of the way, and I tied the two loose ends together. "There, you're perfect." She turned around and indeed she was. Even in her plain servant's dress, she was a sight to behold.

She smiled up at me and tilted her head up

for a kiss. I took her into my arms and kissed her slowly, as if we had all the time in the world. When the kiss ended Latisha looked delightfully flushed and I wanted nothing more than to strip her naked and haul her back to bed.

"Time for breakfast." She held out her hand and we walked together to the servant's dining hall.

"Oh my, are you two a thing now?" Bexi eyed our joined hands. I half expected Latisha to drop my hand and pretend we were merely friends. I wouldn't have blamed her for it. This was all still new for her. But she didn't. She smiled at Bexi and everyone else at the table and just said, "Yep." And I felt two feet taller now that she'd claimed me as hers.

We grabbed our breakfast and sat across from each other at the end of the table. I was in the middle of playing footsie with my beautiful mate when one of those god-awful merchant announcements came on.

"Good morning, citizens. Welcome to another day on our beautiful planet, Ozinda. I wanted to join you at your breakfast table to alert everyone of a new job opportunity. House Dirgach just opened a new mine in the southern Tellag mountain region."

Suddenly the announcement cut out and was replaced with static. "Be ready, rebels. Tonight is the night." A modulated voice came through. "And merchants be warned, none of you are safe anymore."

The message cut off and the room was silent. We waited for the merchant to come back on, but when they never did the room filled with quiet whispers about what the cryptic message could mean. Questions of *where are we meeting*, and *what are we doing*, spread across the room. No one had any answers, not even Vinee, who usually knew everything about the rebellion and their plans. In the past week servants from different districts had been retaliating against the merchants. There had been worker strikes, factories looted, and some merchants have been been driven out of their own homes. Everyone around the table looked eager for their turn to have an active role in the rebellion.

After breakfast Latisha and I parted ways. She went to fulfill her servant's duties and to check on Jaris and I reported to my guard post. Kach was not thrilled that his guest had slipped out during the night.

"I took a short break to relieve my bladder and when I got back your guest was gone." I explained to a furious Kach.

"He was passed out. He shouldn't–couldn't have," he corrected himself, "been able to leave."

"He's a merchant's son, right? Do you think he hired someone to watch out for him in case something like this happened?" I suggested.

Kach nodded his head. "Jaris does have very well-trained friends. They could have gotten into the mortress and gotten him out." Kach looked at me with renewed anger. "I'll be adding another year of servitude to your contract for this failure."

"I understand, sir." I bowed low and tried to look as sad as I possibly could. I wouldn't be here much longer. Once my mate left I'd be gone too.

The rest of the day moved at a glacial pace. It was strange, yesterday evening was the most important life-changing night of my life, and today everyone was moving about as if nothing had happened. I wanted to shout from the rooftops that I had the best mate in the world. I wanted to run to her and carry her to bed where I would pleasure her over and over again until she begged me to stop. But here I was, standing outside Kach's door, counting down the minutes until my shift ended.

Latisha and I had agreed to keep up appearances. She needed to remain undercover to gather intel, which meant that I needed to be a good boy and not cause any trouble.

After what felt like an eternity Crunn arrived to relieve me of my post. He eyed me suspiciously and was a bit jumpy every time I made any sudden moves. Good, I wanted him afraid of me. If fear was what it would take to keep him away from my mate then I'd gladly fill his life with nightmares.

I rushed down the stairs to find Latisha. Most of the servant's evening work was done on the first floor, and I figured I'd find her there. I walked down one hallway and then another until I spotted my mate reaching up to dust a shelf.

I snuck up behind her and pulled her into my arms. "There you are." I buried my face in her hair and breathed in her delectable scent. "It's been agony being separated from you today."

"Has it? I barely missed you at all."

I smiled against her neck. My goddess loved to

taunt me.

"Shall I show you what you've been missing? Shall I plunge my tongue between the folds of your sex and suck on your sweet perilla until you cry my name?"

Her heart rate sped up. *Bump-da-bump-da-bump.* "Yes." The word came out as a breathy moan.

I took her by the hand and had every intention of leading her upstairs where I could pleasure her on a proper bed, but when I smelled her arousal I realized I wouldn't be able to make it that far. We passed a linen closet and I picked her up, placed her on a large pile of sheets, and shut the door behind us. I couldn't wait any longer; I needed to taste my goddess *now.*

I slid my hand under her dress and hooked a finger around her underwear. I locked eyes with hers as I slid the garment down her leg. I pushed the skirt of her dress up to her waist and her breath hitched when I started to kiss up her thigh.

"Are you going to give me a command, my goddess?" She moaned as I kissed and nipped at her legs, but then I stopped before I could reach glistening sex. "I can be a good boy and wait patiently for your decree, but this door doesn't lock and who knows when someone will come in here looking for fresh linens?"

A smile crossed her face. "I guess we better get started then. You will lick me, suck me, and bend me over this pile until I'm panting your name."

"That I can do," I purred.

I licked her pussy until she whimpered and I

sucked her perilla until her legs trembled. Then she gave me the command to bend her over and to show her exactly how badly I needed to be inside her.

I lifted her off her seat then turned her around. I rubbed her back as I undid my pants and let them gather at my ankles.

Grabbing her hips I slicked my hard dick with her essence until neither of us could take it anymore.

"Now, my kira-si. I need you." Right as I was about to plunge into her I spied a horizontal bar that was easily within Latisha's reach.

"Why don't you stand up and grab that bar and don't let go until you can't take any more of me."

Her mouth quirked up in a grin as she understood my meaning. She grabbed the bar that was far enough above her head that she was deliciously stretched out, but not so high that she would have to stand on her tippy-toes.

I slid my cock through her essence once more before entering the paradise that was her pussy. We moaned in unison as I pressed myself deeper and deeper into her channel. Once fully seated, I slid my hand under her dress and worked her nipples, tugging and pinching them until I was satisfied they had received their due attention.

I made my way down to her sex and thrust in and out of her while I worked her sensitive bundle of nerves. Her channel fluttered around me and I moaned at the exquisite pressure of it. Every time I entered my mate it was a new experience of ecstasy. I was once again amazed at how right it felt with her body pressed against mine.

She was mewing and trembling now. I wasn't doing much better as my knees felt weaker with every thrust, my balls heavy and tight.

"Harder," she pleaded and I took it as a command. I thrust hard into her while still working her perilla and she and I both gasped as the sensation reverberated through us. Again and again I thrusted as hard as her pussy could take until I felt that glorious constriction of muscles that surrounded her channel squeezing me so tight I could barely breathe.

Her name spilled from my lips as she gasped mine. I shuttled into her a few more times as my semen filled her to the brim.

We exited the closet a few minutes later looking a bit disheveled, but happy as could be.

"Shall we head down to dinner?" I held out my hand for Latisha.

"That sounds like a good idea." She took my hand and wrapped her tail around mine as we walked.

* * *

Latisha

My mind was galaxies away when I loaded up my dinner plate. I was still thinking about our time in that closet. I could still feel the chill of the metal bar in my hands as I held on while Bowen bucked into me. A sensual chill ran down my spine. We'd just mated a few minutes ago and I already wanted him again.

As if he could read my thoughts, Bowen smiled down at me and added a piece of bread to my plate. We sat down at the table side by side. I shook some spice onto my meat and vegetables.

"May I have the spice shaker?"

"Oh, this one?" I gave it another small shake over my food and then pretended I was going to pass it down the table.

"You better not," Bowen pretended to frown but the tone of his voice told me he was happy to play along.

"Cassia, do you need the spice shaker?" I started to reach out my arm to hand it to her when Bowen snatched it from me.

"I'll take that if you don't mind." He grinned at me as he shook out the seasoning and wrapped his tail around my leg. "Here you go Ms. Cassia." He reached over me and passed it down the table.

Before he pulled back he whispered in my ear, "You're being very naughty."

"*I'm* being naughty? You're the one not following my command."

"Oh, so that was a command now, was it?"

"Yes it was and I'm going to punish you later for not following my orders," I purred in a hushed tone.

Bowen visibly shook as a chill ran down his spine and his tail thumped the floor. "You have no idea how I've longed for you to punish me."

Now it was my tail thumping the floor.

The sound of static coming through everyone's

buzzpads drew my attention away from our conversation.

"Rebels, the time is now! Follow the Sirrets in the Junak masks! Long live the Junak!"

Everyone around the table stopped what they were doing and ran for the exit. Bowen and I joined them outside. The street was dotted with Sirrets wearing replica silver Junak masks running toward the merchant district.

"To house Dirgach! To house Dirgach!" The rebel leaders chanted. Bowen and I looked at each other and took off in a sprint toward the Dirgach mortress. When we arrived the masked rebels were at the gate attaching something to the hinges.

"Down, down, down," one of them yelled. I suddenly felt the full weight of Bowen pushing me down to the ground. A moment later there was a large bang and a small explosion. Shrapnel flew all around us and then it was quiet. Bowen lifted himself off my body and helped me up off the ground. The gates blocking the mortress had been blown off their hinges. One lay on the ground and the other was nowhere to be seen.

Shouts erupted from the crowd and everyone ran past the gate onto the property. The Dirgach servants working at the mortress looked shocked and terrified as rebels swarmed the house. A rebellion leader stood in the middle of the entryway and addressed the them.

"The rebellion is here! Join us or get out of the way!"

Many of the servants dropped their mops and dusters and joined the hoard of people looting and destroying the mortress.

"Dirgach isn't here! He must have slipped out the back," a servant yelled.

"Let him go. We're not here for him, we're here to send a message. Let's raze this building to the ground!"

All around me, people were breaking vases, ripping curtains from their rods, pocketing expensive trinkets, and dismantling the house brick by brick. It was a sight to behold.

"It looks like there's a fire sale going on. Is there anything you'd like before it's all gone?" Bowen had a grin on his face and his green eyes darted back and forth taking in the scene.

"I wouldn't mind taking home a souvenir or two." I winked at him and he barked out a laugh.

We ran up the stairs to see what was left of the bedroom suite. We passed a Dirgach servant emptying out dresser drawers of fine clothes onto the floor.

"I washed his clothes everyday and what was the thanks I got? Nothing. He treated me like dirt just like he treated everyone else." They picked up the clothes off the ground, shoved them out the window and yelled, "take that you pathetic excuse for a Sirret! I'm never going to wash your clothes again!"

"Good for her," Bowen commented.

We made our way down the hallway to a room with a large painting of Norvan in expensive business attire. Next to it was a smaller painting of what I assume was Norvan as a youngling standing next to his mother. He looked so much like her from his facial features right down to his curly hair.

"He was such a sweet boy. It's a shame Dirgach sent his mother away." A servant sat on the bed wiping away tears with her apron. "I only kept working here in hopes that he might return. His mother gave me a note to pass onto him, but I never got the chance."

"You have a note from his mother?" Did I hear her right? Norvan said his mother had to flee or she would have been killed by his father for trying to take Norvan with her when she left Dirgach. Norvan hadn't seen her since.

"Yes she gave it to me a few moons ago. Too bad he's dead." The female wiped away more tears from her face.

"Dead? Norvan's not dead." I corrected her. Bowen furrowed his eyebrows at me. I would have to explain how I knew Norvan later.

"But Dirgach said he was dead. We held a funeral for him and everything." I wonder how Norvan would feel about that.

"He's not dead. He's very much alive and well. He has a mate and a youngling on the way."

"Truly?" The female stood. A mix of relief and shock crossed her face. "Do you know him?"

"We are acquaintances."

"Can you give him this note?" The female handed me a folded piece of paper. I took it and unfolded it. I had expected to see a long letter but instead, it was just an address.

"That's where she lives. Give it to Norvan so he can finally find her. That's all he wanted to do for years is find his mother, but Dirgach kept a close eye on him. That poor boy couldn't get away with anything."

"I'll give it him. You have my word." I promised the elder Sirret. She gave me a small bow and took the painting of Van and his mother off the wall and left the room.

"Are you alright? That was an intense conversation," Bowen asked.

"Yeah I'm okay. I don't really know Norvan that well, but he deserves to know where his mother is." At least he might have a chance at a good relationship with his mom, something I'll never get.

"Let's go back downstairs. Maybe there's something in the basement that we can take with us," Bowen suggested. I nodded my head and he lead the way out of the room.

We walked to the basement and found a group of Sirrets pulling on a thick chain attached to the wall.

A male looked at Bowen and I and pleaded, "Help us, please. He tortured people down here. Even if the house burns down these chains will still be attached to this wall and I can't have that. Never again will anyone be chained down here."

Bowen and I looked at each other and without speaking we took our places in line gripping the thick chain and pulled when everyone else did. After many tries the metal finally detached from the wall.

"We did it!" The servants jumped and cheered.

One held the chain in the air and heaved it across the room.

"Never again." The male that pleaded with us to help declared. "Never again."

"Everybody out! We're blowing the house up!" A Sirret in a silver Junak mask yelled. We all rushed out of the house and ran a good distance down the street.

A rebel in a mask stood on top of a crate and yelled, "The Junak has ordered us to destroy this house. There shouldn't be a single brick left standing. I hope you got everything you wanted out of the house because soon it's going to be gone."

"It's clear! Everyone is out!" A rebel yelled as he ran out of the mortress a safe distance away.

"It's time then." The rebel on the crate pulled out a detonator. "For the rebellion! For the Junak!" He shouted over and over again until the crowd chanted with him.

"Down with Dirgach!" Someone added and soon the street was filled with the sound of rebels declaring war. This was their first major strike. They had bombed factories, blown up space cruisers, and scared other merchants away, but this felt more personal. This was a merchants house, their fortress, their sanctuary and it was about to get blown to pieces.

"Everybody down!" Again Bowen covered me with his body and a loud explosion rang through the air. We were hit with a shockwave that knocked us over then smoke filled the night sky. The crowd stood back up waiting for the smoke to clear. They was an eerie silence that fell over everyone. We waited and waited until flames cut through the smoke illuminating the remains of the house.

It was gone. As the smoke drifted away the fire light up the night sky. The flames shone brighter than the morning sun. It felt like a new day was dawning, a brighter day.

"The peacekeepers are coming! The peacekeepers are coming!" a rebel lookout yelled.

Bowen started tugging me along so we could flee the area, but I needed to know who the Junak was. Why hadn't he shown himself?

"Where is the Junak?" I asked one of the rebellion leaders.

"He's not here tonight. He'll make an appearance in a sun cycle or two."

"Sweetheart, we have to go," Bowen looked about ready to pick me up and throw me over his shoulder. I nodded my head and we ran together down the alley.

After a close call with the peacekeepers, we made it back to the Dinak mortress. I snuck Bowen into the women's dorm and we slept cuddled together in my bed.

CHAPTER 23

Bowen

Lunch the day after the rebellion took down the Dirgach house was both electric and full of sorrow. Everyone seated around the table had taken part in tearing down that house. We felt powerful, unstoppable even. But a handful of servants were missing as well. Servants who had been apprehended by the peacekeepers. The peacekeepers here don't follow any rules of due process. If the guards gave ACAB vibes the peacekeepers were ten times worse. They made the most money of all the laborers, money that kept them loyal to the merchants and no one else.

My heart went out to the servants who had been captured last night. I could only hope they survived the night without getting too roughed up. Ozinda peacekeepers, for all their brutality, at least did their best to not kill their prisoners. *Why kill a prisoner when you could use them for free labor?* was the mantra here. But they didn't hold back anything when it came to beating prisoners.

Latisha squeezed my knee under the table and I gave her a weak smile.

"A lot on your mind?"

I nodded. "Just thinking about everyone who is missing from the table."

"Me too." She looked down at her plate and pushed her food around, not eating any of it.

We both looked up as Vinee ran into the room, panting as if he'd run a marathon. "Dirgach and the peacekeepers have set up a platform in the middle of the city square. They're going to execute some of the rebels they caught last night."

For the second time that week, everyone stopped what they were doing and ran out the door. The whole lot of us ran all the way to the city square where Dirgach was standing on a makeshift platform next to three rebels in chains.

By the time we got there a large crowd had already formed. I looked around and saw a sea of angry Sirret faces. If it weren't for the large peacekeeper presence, I'd wager this crowd would have swarmed Dirgach the moment he stepped up on that platform.

"Oh no, it's Emed and Drav!" I turned to the side and saw Bexi pointing to the chained prisoners. Airna was beside her, clutching Bexi's arm and looking like she'd forgotten how to breathe.

Emed, Drav and another Sirret I didn't recognize were chained to the platform and doing their best not to look scared.

"You think you can tear down my house without consequences?" Dirgach shouted over the crowd. "You think you have the numbers to take me down? Well, go ahead and try. I've got an army of peacekeepers at my back ready to strike."

He stepped toward the Sirret I didn't recognize and was handed a needle gun from a peacekeeper. "This is what's going to happen if you try to take me down. Every time you attack me, I'll kill the prisoners that are captured."

He inserted the needle into the Sirret's arm and pushed the handle down, injecting the liquid. Immediately the Sirret drained of color from their head to their toes. They dropped to the ground, pale and lifeless.

Dirgach moved to young Drav next and he tried to put on a brave face as the peacekeeper held out his arm for Dirgach. Time stood still as the merchant lifted the needle gun to the teenager's skin.

"No!" Young Airna cried and ran toward the platform. All hell broke loose, and the angry crowd turned into a murderous mob. The Sirrets closest to the stage hopped up and freed Emed and Drav from their chains. Rocks and other heavy objects were thrown at Dirgach and his guards before they could flee to the safety of the peacekeepers. The mob tore the stage apart and threw the pieces at the armed force.

"Don't stand there! Shoot them!" Dirgach gave the order and laser fire went flying every which way. I put myself between Latisha and the peacekeepers and we ran to safety. Something hot burned my leg and I fell to my knees with a yelp.

"Bowen!" Latisha's hands steadied me as we both looked at my wound. My thigh had been grazed with laser fire. It wasn't a deep wound but it sure hurt like a motherfucker and it was bleeding much more than a burn wound should. What were these lasers made of?

Latisha helped me up and I leaned on her as I hobbled back to the house as fast as I could. She walked me to Kach's elevator which was supposed to be off-limits, but it was either risk being caught or hobble up four flights of stairs. I'd take my chances. It wasn't much longer before Latisha was helping me into her bed.

"Take off your pants. I need to see the extent of your wound."

"I like it when you're bossy." My words were slurring and my vision had turned fuzzy. I must have lost a lot of blood walking over here.

"This isn't a time for jokes." Latisha sounded panicked.

"Who's joking?" I smirked up at her and she rolled her eyes at me.

As she took off my pants the fabric grazed my wound and pain shot up my leg, making me hiss.

"Sorry," she winced. "At least it's not a deep wound. Stay here and I'll get some medicine and bandages."

"I wasn't planning on going anywhere," I laughed and she rolled her eyes at me again.

I must have dozed off because I didn't remember Latisha returning to the room, but when I looked down my wound was fully wrapped and feeling much better.

"When did you get here?" I yawned.

"Good, you're awake," she breathed a sigh of relief. "I put a salve on the wound and bandaged it up pretty tight. How does it feel?"

"It feels pretty good. You know what would make it feel even better?"

She eyed me suspiciously. "What?"

"If you were laying on this bed with me."

"Bowen, you are wounded." Latisha started to cover me with the blanket.

"And a wounded man needs to rest, so why don't you relax a little and take a nap with me?"

"I'm supposed to be working."

"You think after what happened anyone's working this afternoon? Come on, play hooky with me and take the afternoon off." I lifted the corner of the blanket up to invite her in.

"I do not know what this 'hooky' is but I will take a nap with you if that's what you mean."

"That's all I want, is for my beautiful mate to relax and take a nap with me."

She laid down in bed and her warm body next to mine felt better than any salve she could put on my leg. She was all I ever wanted for now and for always.

* * *

Latisha

Bowen's chest rose and fell with each breath. I hadn't fallen asleep, but it brought me peace to see him resting. I'd never been so afraid in my life than when Bowen fell to the ground with a piercing shriek. My heart had nearly stopped in my chest. I'd just found my mate and in one moment, if that laser fire had been a few hand spans higher, he would have been gone and I could have lost him forever.

I watched his chest rise and fall for the rest of the afternoon. Bexi brought Emed to her bed and they napped as well. He looked shaken. He had been a breath away from death. If the crowd hadn't swarmed the platform I doubt he'd be here now.

Static cut through the silence in the room and Junak's voice came through our buzzpads.

"Fellow rebels. I applaud you for what you did to the Dirgach house and-" the voice modulator cut out and the Junak's real voice came through, "how you saved two of your own from imminent death. Rest today. We will retaliate soon." The message cut off. His voice sounded so familiar, but I couldn't think of who it was.

Bowen stirred next to me. "Did you say something?"

"No, that was the Junak. He was congratulating us on what we did to the Dirgach house."

"Oh, how nice of him." He rolled over and fell back asleep.

The next day Bowen was feeling much better. The medicine reserved for the guards really was powerful stuff. He reported to guard duty and I resumed my normal schedule of chores. I was changing out the sheets in the guest room as I replayed the words from the Junak yesterday. *How you saved two of your own from imminent death. Rest today. We will retaliate soon.*

Over and over I replayed his words in my mind. That voice was so familiar. I *knew* I had heard it before, but from who? Who was the Juank?

By the goddess. It hit me. I knew exactly who that voice belonged to. I ran up the stairs to Kach's bedroom suite. The door was open and Bowen stood outside.

"Is he in there?" I pointed to the door.

"Who?" Bowen's brows furrowed together.

"Kach."

"No, he's taking a meeting in the conference room. It should be wrapping up soon."

I walked past Bowen into the room and immediately started going through Kach's drawers. Just as before, they were empty. His wall safe! I lifted the painting that kept the safe hidden and tried typing in random key codes to open it. Nothing worked. I could really use Drannon's expertise right now.

"What are you doing?" Bowen looked around the room at all the drawers I'd left open.

"It's him." I half-heartedly explained.

"Who?"

"The Junak, Kach is the Junak."

"There's no way. That asshole wouldn't lift a finger to help anybody, much less lead a rebellion." Bowen was dubious.

"It's him. I heard his real voice in the message yesterday."

I pulled a dagger from Bowen's belt and pried open the keypad. Alright, what had Drannon taught me about this stuff? Cut the red wire and cross it with the green one? I did just that and I heard a click.

I looked up at Bowen whose eyes were wide. "Well, go ahead, let's see what's inside."

I opened the vault and inside was a shiny gold Junak helmet. The same one the Junak was wearing last night during his live-streamed speech. I lifted it out of the vault and was surprised by how heavy it was. This was made out of real gold.

Tisk, tisk, tisk. "I wish you wouldn't have done that," A voice said from behind us. I turned to see Kach standing behind Bowen. Crunn and Gonuk stood behind him with phase guns aimed at our heads. We were pinned against the wall with nowhere to run.

"I really liked you two, and now that you know my little secret, neither of you will ever see the light of day again."

CHAPTER 24

Latisha

Kach led us down to the basement and then opened a hidden hatch door set into the floor. We walked down one last flight of stairs until we reached a dimly lit corridor of rooms. At the center was a cell with stone walls and metal bars to block one's escape. Cruun and Gunok shoved us into the cell and locked the gate behind us.

The room was dark and smelled of mildew. There was just one window in the entire room and it was high up on the wall far above anyone's reach. There were a few old blankets on the floor to sit on, but other than that the room was empty.

Kach entered the outer room holding the Junak mask under his arm. He looked us both up and down as we stood behind the bars.

"It's such a shame, really. You both would have been such good rebel leaders," he sighed.

"Why are you doing this? Why are you leading a rebellion when you clearly don't even care about your own servants?" I asked. None of this made sense to me.

"I don't have to like my servants to lead a rebellion," he looked at his nails as if he were bored with our conversation.

"Then why do it? Why pretend to lead them?"

"Oh, I'm not pretending. I am leading them. I've lead them to destroy nearly every merchant house, leaving a nice little power vacuum in their wake."

Kach's motivations became clear. "You're going to make yourself the emperor of Ozinda. You just used these people for your own gain."

Kach smiled down at me. "I knew you were a smart female. Tomorrow I'll reveal myself to my followers and they will bow to me as their ruler."

"Why would they do that? Your servants know who you really are. They would never believe you," I postulated.

"Because I am the savior of the working class, I am the Junak, and what are a handful of dissenters against a multitude of loyal subjects? Besides, they can't spread rumors about me being a bad male if they're in prison now can they?

"So you were going to imprison us anyway, even if you hadn't caught us in your room?" Bowen's face was pinched with anger as he spat out the words.

"Unfortunately, yes, but tonight you'll stay in my dungeon to make sure you don't warn any of the other servants. In fact–Crude, Gunok," he turned to the guards. "interrogate these two. See who else might be suspicious of the Junak's real identity. I wouldn't want anyone to ruin my grand reveal."

With that, Kach went back up the stairs and the door slammed shut behind him.

"I've been waiting a long time to mess you up, Bowen." Crunn's smile was far too wide when he opened the door and yanked Bowen out. "Kach has a very special torture device he's been saving just in case you got out of line," Gunok added.

"Bowen!" I shouted as I reached a hand through the bars. Crunn had Bowen's hands tied behind his back. I couldn't reach him and he couldn't reach me.

"Don't worry sweetheart, I'll be back soon," He tried to smile but he couldn't. The last image I saw of my mate were his ears twitching nervously on the top of his head.

I pulled my transmitter pendant out of my apron pocket and pressed the center of it until the black stone turned red. "Hello, Drannon, I need your assistance. I am currently located in a secret dungeon in Kach's house. There's a whole other floor beyond what the blueprints showed. I am requesting an extraction for myself and a guard named Bowen who is down here with me. I repeat: I need an extraction, the sooner the better."

❈ ❈ ❈

Bowen
CW: Torture via medical equipment

I readied myself for whatever Gunok and Crunn had in store for me. I could take a few punches.

It wasn't like I had a choice, I didn't have any information to share with them. I had learned of the Junak's true identity just a few minutes ago.

We entered a small side room with a hospital bed. There was a bulky piece of equipment to the side of it, but it was covered with a blanket. This was not good. I'd expected to receive a few punches, not to be strapped down to a hospital bed.

"Go ahead and tie him down, Crunn. I'll hold him while you do." *Fuck, fuck, fuck.* I squirmed and tried to break free of Gunok's grip, but he wasn't giving me an inch. They laid me down on the bed and tied my wrists and ankles down to the frame.

"Hey guys, look, I know we haven't been the best of pals in the past, but that doesn't mean we have to betray each other like this. Just untie me, walk me back to the cell, and I'll tell Kach you tortured me. I'll even let you each punch me to make it look real."

Crunn and Gunok looked at each other and laughed. "Oh Bowen, we're aren't going to punch you; in fact, we aren't going to touch you at all."

Crunn pulled the sheet off the machine next to the bed to reveal an expensive vitals monitor, the kind that ticked, the same kind the scientists had used on me.

Panic surged through me. "Guys, I promise I don't know anything. I just found out about Kach being the Junak right before you entered the room."

They ignored my pleas and hooked me up to the machine. I tried to squirm again but I was tied down tight.

"Don't turn that thing on, please," I begged.

Gunok smiled as he turned the knob powering up the machine. *Tick, tick, tick.* That awful high pitched sound filled the room, and memories of pain and unimaginable suffering flooded back to me.

"Tell us who you talked to about the Junak being Kach," Gunok asked.

"I didn't! I just found out moments before you walked into the room!" The ticking was getting impossibly louder in my mind and my ears started to ring.

"I'm sure you had your suspicions though, why else would you be looking around his room?" At this point I couldn't tell who was asking me questions. All the sounds blurred together except for that damn ticking.

"I just had a hunch, that was all. I didn't talk to anyone." I didn't have a hunch. Latisha had figured it out, but I would never tell them that. They didn't need a reason to torture her, too.

"Just a hunch, huh? Why don't we leave you alone in here with your favorite medical equipment and let you think about who you may have talked to about Kach and the Junak?"

"No!" I thrashed against my restraints. They couldn't leave me in here. I could already feel myself slipping away into madness. I was losing myself to the memories the ticking brought back. For months I would lie on a bed just like this one and feel like nothing more than a conscious ameba as my body painfully grew new fur, new ears, an altered nose, and paws where my feet used to be. All the while I didn't know who I was or who I'd been. My brain had turned to mush while my body shifted from human to katsuro. I had lost all grip on reality. My mind was filled with a dark void that I didn't think I'd ever get out of.

Tick, tick, tick, tick... I tried to fight it but I could feel the darkness overpowering me once again.

CHAPTER 25

Latisha

I banged against the metal bars every time I heard Bowen screaming. I couldn't imagine what they were doing to my mate. He was always so calm and collected; what sinister torture could they be forcing upon him to make him scream like that?

After what felt like day cycles Crunn and Gunok dragged Bowen back to our cell. He was mumbling to himself and he couldn't even walk. They dumped him on the floor and locked the gate behind them.

"Bowen," I shook him, but he didn't respond. He was trembling all over and was soaked with sweat.

"Bowen," I shook him again, but all I got was incoherent mumbling.

"Bowen," I sobbed, tears streaming down my face. What had they done to him? What had they done to my mate?

Feeling helpless, I sat down and rested my back against the wall. I pulled Bowen onto my lap and ran my fingers through his hair.

"Please come back to me," I begged. "I don't

know how to fix this."

I held him in my arms and rocked back and forth trying to soothe him. His song might work. I tried to remember the words to his sunshine song.

"*You are my sunshine, my only sunshine. You make me happy when skies are gray. You'll never know dear how much I love you, so please don't take my sunshine away.*"

He stopped trembling and I kept singing. I laid his head back onto my lap and kept running my fingers through his hair.

"Please, Bowen, you are my sunshine. I know I'm prickly. I'm nothing but dark clouds and gray skies, but you are the sunshine that penetrates my storm. I need you Bowen, please. I need your sunshine."

I wept as I ran my fingers through his hair. My tears soaked my skin and I did my best to sing his sunshine song through my sobs. I needed him. I needed him to come back to me.

❊ ❊ ❊

Bowen

You are my sunshine my only sunshine... There was a voice in the darkness. *You are my sunshine my only sunshine...* A light appeared high above me. The voice drew me toward it, away from the darkness. *You make me happy when skies are gray.* I opened my eyes and saw a goddess with broken black horns. *You'll never know dear how much I love you.* She was so beautiful. *Please don't take my sunshine away.* She was crying. Why was she crying? Who would make a goddess cry?

I felt a strong urge to protect her. I needed to keep her safe but I felt so weak all I could do was reach up and wipe the tears away from her face.

"Don't cry, sweetheart." My voice sounded raspy and distant.

"Bowen!" The goddess scooped me up in her arms and squeezed me tight. "You're back. You came back to me."

"Who would leave a goddess?"

"You did. They took you and then when they brought you back you weren't responding to me."

"They took me?" Fuzzy memories started to come back. Two men–no not men, Sirrets–took me to a room. They wanted me to tell them something. I refused and they strapped me down and then there was the ticking, so much ticking, and then the darkness came.

"Latisha." I cupped her cheek in my hand. My mate, my goddess, my everything. I was coming back to myself and remembering who I was.

"What did they do to you?" Her face was wet. She'd been crying for me. That more than anything made me want to go on a rampage. Do what you want with me, but hurt Latisha? They were going to pay for that.

"They hooked me up to the same medical equipment the scientists used. It brought back bad memories."

Latisha nodded, settled my head back down on her lap, and ran her fingers through my hair. "I'm going to make them pay when we get out of here," she promised.

"Should we attack them when they move us to the prison?" I didn't have my knives on me, but my claws would work just fine.

"I called in an extraction. Someone from my team should be able to get us out of here before Kach tries to move us."

"I like your security job. It comes with nice perks," I smiled up at her.

"I'm glad you like it," she chuckled.

I closed my eyes and basked in the feeling of Latisha's hands on me. "I'm just going to close my eyes for a minute," I told her.

"Sleep, Bowen, you need it." And I did just that.

When I next opened my eyes I saw morning light shining through the small window high up on the wall.

"Latisha?" I panicked when I didn't see my mate. She wasn't in front of me. I sat up and immediately felt dizzy.

"Latisha!"

"I'm right here." I heard a groggy voice from behind me.

"Oh," I gave her a sheepish smile and a kiss on the cheek. "I guess I'm still not with it. When I didn't see you in front of me I assumed the worst."

"I'm here. I'll always be here." She smiled and all my fears faded away. She had called for an extraction and they'd be here soon, at least that's what I kept telling myself.

"I had dreams last night of you singing to me. Did that really happen?" My memories of yesterday were still fuzzy.

"Yeah, that happened. I didn't know what to do when you wouldn't respond to me, so I sang your sunshine song." She looked down and tucked her hair behind her ear.

"Oh, don't be bashful, now. You have a great singing voice," I teased her.

"That was a one-time thing. There will be no more singing," she blushed a delicious dark blue.

I pulled her onto my lap and kissed her gently. "When we get out of here, and I get you back into a bed, I bet I can make you sing again."

"Bowen!" She slapped my shoulder. "We are in a dungeon! How can you think about that."

"When it comes to you, I'm always thinking about that," I purred.

Our playful banter was interrupted by the door slamming. Crunn and Gonuk walked in and the panic I felt yesterday started to creep back in.

Crunn unlocked the gate. "Alright female, it's your turn today."

"No!" I growled as I stepped between Latisha and Crunn. The movement left me dizzy, but I fought through it. "You will not take her," I growled.

"It turns out you don't have much of a choice in this." Gonuk slid a strange-looking rod through the metal bars and as soon as it touched my skin I yelped in pain and fell to the floor. It was the Feno version of a taser and it hurt. Before I could get back up they had taken Latisha out of the cell and locked the gate again.

CHAPTER 26

Latisha

"Don-don't yo-you touch ha-her!" Bowen shouted from our cell. The eclectic pulse rod had messed him up pretty bad. I looked back and he was gripping the bars and barely able to stand.

"Bowen!" I wanted to run back to him. He was hurt. He needed me and I needed him.

"Latisha!" He wailed my name as the guards continued to pull me away. They led me to an empty side room that had a table and chairs inside.

"We're going to tie you down just to make sure you don't try anything." One guard held me down while the other tied a rope around my wrists and ankles, securing me to a chair.

"I don't suppose you know anything, do ya?" Crunn licked his lips as he eyed me.

"She's a female servant. She was probably just in the room when Bowen opened the vault." They talked about me as if I wasn't sitting right in front of them.

"Why did you bring me in here?" I wasn't exactly eager to learn what torture they had in store for me, but I also didn't want to put off the inevitable.

"Well, we're not going to torture you, if that's what you're asking," Gonuk pulled out a fume stick and took a puff of vapor.

"You're not?" This was welcome news but why bring me back here if they weren't going to question me?

"No, We suspect Bowen is holding back information so we brought you here to get him to talk."

"Let's see how it's working." Crunn opened the door.

"Don't touch her, you bastards! I swear to god I'll burn this whole place down! Don't touch–" Crunn shut the door again.

"I'd say it's going pretty well wouldn't you, Gonuk?" Crunn laughed.

The guards stayed in the room with me for a while longer before going back to Bowen. As I sat there alone wondering what kind of lies they were telling my mate I pondered if there was any information I could give them, true or false. It was to my benefit that they saw me as a dumb female, but that wasn't helping Bowen at all, and I was the reason he was down here.

The guards came back looking rather surly. "Come on female, let's go." They untied me and led me back to my cell.

"What happened?" I couldn't help but ask. This torture idea had ended up being very short-lived.

"That biffing catman has gone crazy. Not only

will he not give us any information, I'm not even sure if he's listening to our questions," Crunn huffed.

"He just keeps screaming for you and demanding your return. The male is truly crazy," Gonuk added.

I held back a smile. It served them right for trying to separate us. I just hoped that my mate was in a better condition than yesterday.

Bowen was sitting against the wall facing away from the bars when they opened the gate. I moved toward him. He was mumbling to himself again.

"I'll destroy those fuckers if they do anything to her."

The guards slammed the gate closed and Bowen got up and clenched his fists ready to fight. As soon as he saw me he relaxed and pulled me tight against his chest.

"Did they do anything to you?" He inspected every inch of me, making sure I was alright.

"They didn't touch me. They only brought me back there to try to get information out of you," I assured him.

"Thank god." He pulled me in again and buried his nose in my hair. "I would have burned this whole house down if they had done anything to you."

"I know," I rubbed my hand up and down his back, soothing him. "I know you would have."

I got more and more nervous as it drew closer to the afternoon. Where was Drannon? If he didn't get here soon Kach would be moving us to the prison. Bowen had calmed down again. I told him to sleep until the effects of the electric pulse rod fully wore off. At first he refused. He wanted to be alert to protect me. Our compromise was that he'd sleep on my lap, and I'd alert him to any danger coming our way.

Tap, tap, tap. I looked up and saw someone outside the window. *Thump, thump, thump, woosh.* The window was pulled free from the frame and pulled backward.

Drannon stuck his head through the opening. "Someone call for an extraction?"

Jaris poked his head in next to Drannon's. "Sorry it took so long. The location of this place is well hidden."

I let out a sob of joy. They were here, Bowen and I were free.

Bowen stirred awake and jumped to his feet. "Who's there?!"

"It's okay. My team is here, they're going to get us out." I pointed up to the window and Jaris and Drannon waved at my mate.

Looking a little shell-shocked, Bowen waved back. "It's nice to see you on your feet. You weren't lookin' too good last time I saw you," my mate commented.

"I'm doing much better, thanks to you," Jaris called down.

Drannon lowered a collapsible ladder down into our cell.

Bowen stood at the bottom holding it steady and motioned for me to start climbing. I made quick work of climbing up the rungs and Bowen climbed up right behind me.

"I can't express how grateful I am to the two of you. Who knows what would have happened had I stayed in that room." Jaris pulled us through the window.

"I still don't understand why he did that. Kach is your oldest friend," Drannon added as he collapsed his portable ladder and placed it in his backpack.

"I know why," I commented as I brushed the dust off my servant's uniform. "Kach is the Junak."

Jaris and Drannon stopped what they were doing and looked up at me with their jaws hanging open.

"I–How? Why?" Jaris stuttered out.

"He's creating a power vacuum. He used the rebels to take out the other merchant houses to make him the last one standing. He's going to reveal himself as the savior of the rebels and make himself emperor."

"He needed me out of the way to make sure I didn't come back to Ozinda and mess up his plan. No wonder he was constantly asking me where I was. He was trying to take me out," Jaris pondered out loud. "What happened to him? He used to be such a good person."

"I don't think he was ever a good person. I think he just pretended to be one in front of you and perhaps the other merchants," I corrected as we started to walk down the alley leading away from the mortress.

"Yeah, your friend is an asshole," Bowen added.

"Noted." Jaris looked thoughtful as he took in this new information.

We quickly made our way to the safe house and I'd never been so relieved to step through a threshold. The weight of everything we'd just been through seemed to fade away as soon as we walked through the door. We were safe.

"Latisha!" Anna ran down the stairs and launched herself at me, encircling me in a tight hug.

Usually I would tense and back away but I didn't feel the need to do that anymore. I embraced her back. She was my friend–or at least, I'd like her to be.

"I have returned." I patted Anna on the shoulder and after a long moment, let go of her embrace.

"Are you alright? Did they hurt you?"

"I am well. They assumed I didn't know anything and left me alone." I let out a sigh of relief and pulled off my bandana. Everyone's eyes went wide.

"Oh my god! Your horns! They're black!" Anna pointed out. "Wait! That means you found your mate. Is this him?" She shifted her attention to Bowen and I had the strange urge to step in front of him to block Anna's view. He was mine. *Calm yourself Latisha. Anna does not want him, she's only asking a question.*

"Yes, everyone meet Bowen, my mate." I took his hand in mine and twisted my tail around his. *Mine.*

"That's so exciting!" Anna clapped her hands in the way her and Maggie did when they were excited. Claire wasn't as expressive. She was more likely to smile at you from a distance.

"Come upstairs. I have a room ready for you." Anna looked at Bowen and corrected herself. "I mean for you and your mate." She grinned at us as if she had brought us together herself. Humans were so strange.

CHAPTER 27

Bowen

"...and that's when Kach walked in on me holding the Junak mask." Latisha filled everyone in on the intel she had gathered at Kach's mortress.

"I never liked that guy. He always had a weird snide comment to make about me when Jaris wasn't around," Anna added.

"You never told me that." Jaris wrapped his tail around Anna's leg and looked hurt by her confession.

"Well, he's your childhood friend. I figured maybe I was reading too much into it or maybe it was a cultural thing."

"That doesn't discount how he made you feel. If any of my acquaintances make you feel like anything less than the amazing female you are, then you tell me about it." He lifted her chin with his finger so her eyes would meet his. "Promise me."

"Ok, I promise," she smiled.

"Good." He turned to my mate. "Now, tell me again what his reasons were for leading the rebellion."

"He wanted to take out all the other merchants so he could more easily step up as the emperor of

Ozinda."

Jaris' brows drew together in a thoughtful expression. "That still leaves Dirgach. The rebels may have burned down his fortress, but he's still alive and running his mines and other businesses. All the other merchants have been driven out of Ozinda or killed."

"I'm glad we were able to get you out of that dungeon before Kach could proceed with any more of his plans." The large Sirret man with the metal legs conveyed his gratefulness as he stood next to his very small human mate. I didn't know how he could touch her without breaking her. I looked over at my mate who was just a few inches shorter than me, the perfect height. Everything about her was perfect.

Static coming from everyone's buzzpads interrupted our conversation.

"Hello citizens of Ozinda!" The Junak, who we now know was Kach, stood on the roof of a building that had the secret construction project clearly in the background. A large holowall blocked the view of whatever was being built next to the mountain range.

"This rotation is one that will be remembered for many years to come. The rebellion has taken down nearly every mighty merchant on Ozinda. You all did a wonderful job destroying Dirgach's house, but I wanted to take things a step further."

Guards wearing replica Junak helmets came into view. They shoved a Sirret with a hood over his head next to Kach.

"Today will mark the end of House Dirgach." The Junak ripped off the hood covering the male's head to reveal Dirgach himself tied up and gagged. "You will harm the Sirret laborers no more!" The Junak took a phase gun out of its holster and without a second of hesitation shot Dirgach in the heart. The room was silent. It felt like the world was silent. We'd just witnessed an execution on a livestream.

"Long live the Junak! Long live the Juank!" The rebels surrounding the Junak chanted.

Kach took off the Junak helmet, revealing his true identity. "No longer will I be known as Kach Dinak. Kach died when the rebellion started. No, from here on out I will be known as the Junak, Emperor of Ozinda!"

Shouts erupted from those who surrounded him. The holowall faded away to reveal a large arena with stadium seating that resembled a football stadium.

"Jaris, can you hear me?" An unfamiliar voice came through Jaris' comm. "Something strange is going on at the secret construction site. We just finished the project and now all the doors are shutting on us. We can't get out!"

"That's Toran, he's the final member of our team," Latisha clarified for me.

"As my first act as emperor," Kach continued. "I present to you the great arena! I have locked up every Sirret I could find who opposed the rebellion. These traitors will serve their time in the prison below the arena, and once their final day has come they will fight to the death like the animals they are!"

"Oh my god," Anna whispered as her hand

covered her mouth in shock.

"Jaris, I'm requesting an extraction! I'll try to get my construction crew to safety, but I'll need your help getting us out of here."

"Toran, run!" A female voice came through the transmitter, and then the message was cut off.

"They're jamming the signal!" Drannon was hunched over the Sirret version of a computer frantically typing in commands.

"I can't get past the encryption." Claire was at her own computer trying to patch Toran back through.

"Well done, my good and loyal rebels. You've earned this reward. You've won and I as your Emperor promise to bring you into a time of prosperity."

"Well, fuck," I cursed as the video feed cut off.

The End

EPILOGUE

Latisha
CW: Conversation about infertility

"What color are you going to pick, Latisha?" Maggie, Norvan, and their youngling Norie had joined us at the safe house on Ozinda. Anna had declared we needed a girl's night to get our minds off Kach and his coup. Toran was still missing, but Drannon and Claire were trying to get past the encrypted communication jammer every day while Jaris and Norvan walked the perimeter of the arena searching for any weak points.

"I will choose the black paint." I held up the small tube of nail paint Claire had brought back from the Sion 6 space station.

"Oh, good choice," Anna congratulated me as if I had solved a great puzzle. I would be annoyed but I was starting to get used to Anna and her overly kind compliments.

"Thank you. You have also chosen well." I pointed to the tube of light purple paint in her hands.

"Thanks! It matches my jumpsuit," Anna smiled.

"What do you think of this blue?" Maggie asked

the group. Norie had fallen asleep after nursing and now she was being held by Norvan who was in the other room. He was eager to show off his progeny as soon as they'd entered the apartment. Everyone oohed and awed over baby Norie and her pale blue skin and brown curly hair. Her eyes were gray like her father's but they had a brown ring around the pupil that was the same shade as Maggie's. I had to admit baby Norie was cute. Maggie said Bowen and I could be an honorary aunt and uncle. Bowen had explained those were familial relationships between siblings and their progeny on Earth. I agreed to the role of aunt. I thought it would be fun to watch little Norie grow up.

"I think that shade would look good on you." Claire was already painting her nails a holographic shade of purple.

Anna had explained that we could paint each other's nails or choose to paint our own. I preferred to paint my own, as did Claire, which meant that Anna and Maggie were free to paint each other's nails, which they preferred. I had often thought this group of humans were just strange beings full of laughter and endless conversation, but now I understood they were a unit that problem-solved and compromised to make sure everyone was comfortable and happy.

"I can't believe that you were only pregnant for five months," Anna commented as Maggie painted her nails.

"I know, right? Norie was a healthy five pounds eight ounces when she was born, which is around the average birth weight for a Sirret baby."

"She's so cute. I can't wait for Jaris and I to have one just like her," Anna mused.

"Have you started the fertility drugs yet?" Claire asked as she held her hand up to the light inspecting her work.

"I was about to start another round of medicine, but then I got the call Jaris was in trouble, and now it feels too risky to get pregnant with Kach's weird kingdom he's trying to build. I think I'll just wait until we can get Toran and go back to Orus 3."

"What about you, Latisha? Are you and Bowen interested in having kids?" Anna's question was innocent enough, but it still made me nervous whenever anyone asked me that. The women still didn't know I was an allgender, or about my infertility. I might tell them eventually, but our friendship is still too new.

Claire must have sensed my hesitation. She cut in, "Dran and I are going to wait. We really like staying busy with our maintenance work, and it's hard to baby-proof a workshop," she laughed. "And you know it's ok to not want kids at all. I don't know how Sirrets feel about being childfree, but I personally think that choosing not to have children can be a great life choice. To each their own and all that."

Anna and Maggie both nodded their heads in agreement.

"Bowen and I prefer to be childfree," I confessed.

"My new friends all smiled at me and the

conversation moved on. I was happy they didn't dwell on the subject.

A knock sounded at the door and Bowen peeked his head in. "Mind if I join you?"

"This is a girl's night, Bowen! You more than anyone should understand that no boys are allowed." Anna blew on her painted nails.

"Yes, but your girl's night is taking too long and I miss my beautiful mate," he pouted. I perked up as soon as he entered the room. I enjoyed the human girl time, but I missed my mate too. Our bond was still new and I still craved him every time we had to be separated.

"That sounds like a *you* problem," Claire said in her flat sarcastic tone I'd come to appreciate.

"You're telling me that if I crashed your girl's night, you'd turn me away?" Drannon popped his head through the door as well and Bowen took that as his chance to sit behind me on the floor.

"I didn't say that," Claire blushed. Drannon also took a seat behind his mate.

"Well if Bowen and Drannon are going to crash the girl's night then I'm certainly not going to sit in the hallway missing my mate either." Jaris strode into the room, sat on a chair and lifted Anna onto his lap.

"We couldn't have that," she purred in his ear.

"Norie and I don't want to be left out, either." Norvan entered the room with baby Norie swaddled in a soft tan blanket and sat in the chair directly behind Maggie.

"Of course not." Maggie smiled at them both

and leaned back against Norvan.

"Well, now that the girls night is thoroughly crashed, I know you ladies won't mind if I steal Latisha away." Bowen stood up and held out his hand for me.

"I certainly do mind," Anna spoke up. She glanced at me and sighed, "It's up to Latisha. If she wants to leave then she can leave, and judging by the smile on her face I can see this is a losing battle."

I was smiling. I was wrapped in my mates arms and I was about to stolen away to what would likely be a long night of pleasure.

"I'm feeling rather tired myself," Claire added with the fakest-looking yawn I'd ever seen. "Dran, will you help me up? I think I'd like to turn in early."

A knowing smile spread across Drannon's face. "Of course, it's important you get a good amount of sleep every night."

"I wouldn't mind spending some time with Van while Norie sleeps," Maggie admitted.

"Well, if everyone else is going to go to their separate bedrooms to fuck the night away, I guess we might as well too." Everyone laughed and Anna lifted Jaris' chin and kissed him as if no one was in the room.

"Come on, sweetheart, let's retire to a more private space," Bowen whispered in my ear.

I nodded my head and my stomach did flip-flops. He didn't know it, but I had a surprise for Bowen waiting in our bedroom.

* * *

Bowen

I couldn't wait any longer. It was hard to be separated from my mate for any length of time, and somehow knowing she was in the next room over only made it worse. Speaking with the Sirrets on Jaris' security team was all fine and well, but it was Latisha I wanted.

The scent of her arousal permeated the air as we walked down the hallway to our room. She had a devious gleam in her eye and her tail swished lazily behind her. Did she have something planned already?

"Have you been a good boy today? Did you play nice with the other males while I was gone?" She purred the question as I shut and locked the door behind us.

"You tell me." I pulled her against me and ran my hand down her side to her supple ass and gave it a good squeeze. "Which is better; the prize for being a good boy or the punishment for being a bad one?"

"You're in luck," she answered as she pulled my shirt off over my head. "You'll get the same treatment either way."

My tail thumped the floor. I started to pull Latisha's shirt off but she batted my hand away.

"Not yet." She unbuttoned my pants and my very hard cock emerged, ready for her pleasure.

"What would you have me do, my goddess? How can I worship you today?" I stepped out of my pants as they fell to the floor.

"Lay down on the bed for me. I've got a surprise

for you." I obeyed her command and laid on the bed like a good boy.

Latisha grabbed a box that had been hiding under the bed. "I grabbed this when I went to the market with Anna today." She lifted a sleek black strap-on cock out of the box and my dick twitched at the sight of it.

"You spoil me too much," I breathed.

"That may be true, but it's just as much a treat for me to see you come undone as it is for you to experience it."

"I don't know about that. I believe I'm about to experience more pleasure than any man deserves."

"Be a good boy and let me be the judge of that," she winked.

"Yes, ma'am."

Latisha fixed the strap on to a comfortable place on her waist. She turned around and commanded, "Fasten this for me."

I did as I was told and then laid back down on the bed. She sat down next to me and placed a gentle hand on my cock and slowly stroked it up and down.

"Kiss me, my kira-si." I had come to learn that was an old Sirret term for a mate, and I loved it. I loved being Latisha's mate. I placed a hand behind her head and drew her toward my lips. The kiss started out as slow and sweet, but then she pulled my bottom lip into her mouth and sucked, which she knew drove me wild. After that, my lips hungrily crashed down on hers. She stroked me harder and moved her other hand to anus. She drew lazy circles around it and gently probed it with her thumb until she was satisfied my body was ready to receive her.

Latisha stood washed her hands with hand sanitizer and pulled a bottle of lube out of the box. She locked eyes with me as she squeezed a generous amount on her hands and rubbed it up and down the phallic object strapped to her abdomen.

My cheeks clenched in anticipation of the pleasure I was about to receive.

"Bend your legs open at the knees." Her words were gentle but there was a fire in her eyes. She was as excited for this as I was.

She crawled onto the bed and lined the strap on with my entrance. My heart was pounding. It had been a while since I'd been topped and I knew without a doubt being pegged by my goddess would be better than anything else I'd experienced prior. Everything was better with her.

She poured more lube on her palm and stroked the strap-on again. "Are you ready for me?"

"Yes," I gulped. I was more than ready.

She lined it up with my entrance again and slowly pushed her way in.

"Ah-ahhhh." My brain shorted out as I felt the delicious pressure of the faux cock inside my body.

"Does it feel good?" Latisha checked in with me.

"So good. So, so good," I assured her.

"I figured we would start out slow," she commented as she slowly pulled back out of me and slowly slid back in.

I gasped and my hips lifted off the bed when

she was fully inside me again. "So, so good." I uttered again between panting breaths.

Latisha started a slow rhythm of gliding in and out as I fisted the sheets enjoying every thrust.

"I have another treat for you," she purred.

"What's that?" I could barely speak the words between my panting. My balls were already so tight, but I desperately wanted this to last as long as possible.

"Lay back and close your eyes." She gently pushed down on my chest until I was laying flat on my back. The sensation of her thrusts with my eyes closed became more and more amplified. Then I felt her rough hand on my cock and I nearly came right then.

"Latisha!" I gasped.

"Let me guess. It feels so, so good," she laughed. Knowing how much she was enjoying this only added to my pleasure.

I couldn't utter words anymore. All I could do was nod my head.

She pumped her hand on my cock in time with her thrusts and my whole world went fuzzy. My fists were clenching the blanket so hard my hands started to hurt. I wasn't going to last much longer. Never had anything felt as good as this. I wanted to tell Latisha how amazing she was, how good this felt, but I couldn't form words. I couldn't concentrate past the dual sensation of the cock inside me lighting up every nerve it touched and the added pleasure of Latisha's hand pumping on my hard, sensitive cock.

Latisha sped up her movements and I trembled, aching for release. Every stroke, every thrust was unimaginably good. I was moaning her name and whining under the waves of pleasure my mate was bringing me.

"Why don't you be a good boy and come for your goddess?" Her voice was deep, raspy, and all-around perfect.

I could hold back no longer. My body went rigid as my orgasm shot through me like a bullet train. I came with a shout and thrust my hips upward as she squeezed the last of my pleasure out of me.

I was a trembling mess on the bed when Latisha exited my body with a self-satisfied smirk.

"God damn!" I ran my fingers through my hair trying to piece myself back together. "As soon as we get a place of our own, I'm going to mount that thing in a display case and put a plaque under it that says *Best Night of Bowen's Life*."

"So does that mean you liked it?" Latisha smiled at me already knowing the answer.

"You know I did," I smiled back.

She stood, undid the fastener, and cleaned the strap-on in the sink of the bathroom that conjoined our room with Drannon and Claire's.

I followed her and hugged her from behind. "You are such a gift."

She wiggled her ass against my cock, and it immediately responded by growing hard again. "Why don't you show me exactly how much you enjoyed your surprise?"

* * *

Latisha

As soon as I shut off the water, Bowen lifted me into his arms and carried me back to the bed. I threw the strap-on into the box right before he shredded my clothes to pieces. His claws were out and he was feral.

"I'm going to make you pay for that," I chided.

"I hope so," he smiled.

He climbed on the bed and laid down on his back. He bent and extended his finger in a come here motion.

I climbed onto the bed next to him and he positioned me with one leg on either side of his body and pushed me forward until my sex hovered over his face.

I swallowed hard. This was not a common Sirret position. I didn't know how long I could sit here on my knees holding myself up over Bowen's face.

"Sit," he growled.

"Sit? On your face? Isn't that dangerous? What if you can't breathe?"

"Then I'll die happy. Now sit, woman!" The command in his tone sent a shiver down my spine. I loved the eager look in his eyes every time he saw my naked body. Today he was even more feral than usual and I loved it.

I slowly lowered myself down until Bowen growled, grabbed my hips, and shoved my wet sex into his own face.

I moaned as he licked up and down my slit, drinking in every drop of wetness he could find. He worked his way up to my perilla and my hips bucked when he took my sensitive flesh into his mouth and sucked. For a moment I didn't know where to place my hands. My thighs? My knees? Eventually, one hand settled on the headboard while the other grabbed Bowen's hair. He moaned as soon as I pulled on his thick hair.

It wasn't long before I was panting and my legs were trembling. I could feel my climax building up inside me, that sweet warmth that pooled in my core and filled my chest. Bowen lifted one hand to my breast and toyed with my sensitive nipple. My hips thrust again and he growled with pleasure, the sensation only added to the orgasm bubbling inside me.

I experimentally ground my sex against his face and he pinched my nipple harder in response. My mate was full of surprises.

I ground down on him again and he sucked even harder. His hand on my breast and mouth on my sex had me whimpering and begging for more. Then suddenly I was on my back, my legs in the air and Bowen's cock hovering at my entrance.

"You want more? I will give you more," he grunted. I nodded my head enthusiastically and he rested my legs up on his shoulders. He pushed inside of me and we both gasped.

He wasted no time on building up with slow

thrusts. This was hard and feral. He gritted his teeth as he pistoned into me. I could feel my climax building up quickly again. Each thrust sent a new set of sensations down my core. Every raised stud on his cock was a dream come true. I was so close now.

He reached down and flicked his thumb back and forth over my bundle of nerves in quick succession. My back arched off the bed and I clenched the bedsheets as my core expanded and retracted with one spasm after another, sending waves of release through my body.

Bowen kept working my perilla and thrusting into my sex as he wrung a second orgasm out of me. This one was bigger than the last. Every nerve was being shredded with pleasure, stitched back together, then rendered apart all over again. I felt as if I had ascended into the heavens and met the goddess herself. For surely she would be here in this place of pure bliss.

I heard a guttural cry and felt Bowen's last thrusts before my legs fell back down onto the bed and he collapsed beside me.

We laid there next to each other, panting. I put my hand on his chest and he placed his hand on top of mine.

"My kira-si," I smiled at my handsome, perfect mate.

"My goddess," he smiled back and tucked my hair behind my ear.

He had my whole heart, every piece. I trusted him and he trusted me.

art by Tainah Ferreira

Glossary

Feno Galaxy - A Galaxy far far away from Earth.

Rut - seasonal rut that Sirret males go through every six months and Sirret women go through once a month.

Bif/biffing - bif is the Feno galaxy's version of fuck

Kira-si (Kira-sye) - old Sirret word for mate

Junak - old Sirret word for savior

Allgender - the Sirret word for an intersex person

Characters:

Norvan (Van) - The only son of House Dirgach. His hobbies are exercising, combat training, and taking care of the livestock on his and Maggie's farm. Mated to Maggie.

Maggie - Wisconsin farm girl, abducted from Earth, given free farm on Orus 3. Loves life. Mated to Van.

Anna Tinsdale - human woman abducted from Earth. Mated to Jaris Hart.

Jaris Hart (Jar-iss) - Sirret Male. Only child of the house of Hart, a wealthy merchant family. He has social anxiety. His mother died when he was young. Mated to Anna Tinsdale.

Kach (catch) - Jaris' best friend, aristocrat

Toran - Sirret Male. The young wild card of the security team. He is currently trapped in Kach's newly built arena. Unmated.

Drannon - Sirret Male. Runs the tech operation of the security team and is the pilot. He has cybernetic legs. Unmated.

Claire - Human woman abducted from Earth.
Latisha - highly sought-after stealth agent. Works for Jaris' security team. Mated to Bowen.
Bowen - Former human turned into a Katsuro-Human hybrid. A little crazy. Mated to Latisha.
Madeline - Human woman abducted from Earth. She was working with a construction team on a secret job site. She is currently trapped in Kach's newly built area. Unmated.

Places:

Ozinda - Prosperous planet in the Feno Galaxy. There are two classes of Sirret people who live there, the uber-wealthy and the very poor.
Orus 3 - Newly terraformed planet. Location of Jaris and Anna's safe house. Location of Maggie and Van's farm.

Thanks For Reading!

Hello dear readers and fellow alien lovers! Thank you for reading Lunar Chaos! I hope you enjoyed Latisha and Bowen's story! Stay tuned for Toran and Madeline's story next.
Please consider leaving a review in Amazon or Goodreads. If you haven't read the other books in the series, I highly suggest you do so!

Crystal Rose Books

Lunar Paradise - Jaris & Anna
Lunar Luxury - Maggie & Norvan
Lunar Joy - Claire & Drannon

Let's Be Friends!

I am most active on instagram at crystalrose.author